Adored

By Nicole Edwards (cont.)

The Devil's Bend Series

Chasing Dreams
Vanishing Dreams

The Devil's Playground Series

Without Regret
Without Restraint

The Office Intrigue Series

Office Intrigue
Intrigued Out of the Office
Their Rebellious Submissive

The Pier 70 Series

Reckless
Fearless
Speechless
Harmless

The Sniper 1 Security Series

Wait for Morning
Never Say Never
Tomorrow's Too Late

The Southern Boy Mafia Series

Beautifully Brutal
Beautifully Loyal

Standalone Novels

A Million Tiny Pieces
Inked on Paper

Writing as Timberlyn Scott

Unhinged
Unraveling
Chaos

Naughty Holiday Editions

2015
2016

Adored

Club Destiny, Book 10

NICOLE EDWARDS

Nicole Edwards Limited
PO Box 806
Hutto, Texas 78634
www.NicoleEdwardsLimited.com

Adored – A Club Destiny novella is a work of fiction. Names, characters, businesses, places, events and incidents either are the products of the author's imagination or used in a fictitious manner. Any resemblance to actual persons, living or dead, business establishments, events, or locales is entirely coincidental.

Cover Images by: © Leung Cho Pan (ID: 12191834) | 123rf.com
Cover Design by: Nicole Edwards Limited
Editing: Blue Otter Editing

ISBN (ebook): 978-1-939786-43-2
ISBN (print): 978-1-939786-44-9

Erotic Romance

Mature Audience

Chapter *One*

"One week? Really?"

Tag smirked at McKenna. Sometimes his fiancée amused him to no end.

Like now, when she was glaring back at him, pure disbelief backlighting her beautiful eyes.

"One week. That's all," he informed her.

McKenna sighed. "Fine. I'm sure I can get Whisper to cover the office without me for a week. I'm just gonna need advance notice so I can—"

"We leave first thing in the morning," Tag told her sternly, fighting a grin.

The look she cast his way would've likely incinerated a lesser man. But Tag had been with McKenna long enough—close to two years now—to expect those fiery looks, especially when he sprung something on her that would take her away from work for longer than a minute.

McKenna owned and operated *Sensations, Inc.*—her well-known online magazine geared toward swingers and the sexually taboo. It wasn't unusual for her to work in excess of seventy hours a week. In fact, it was rare that she didn't. McKenna had been highly successful before he'd met her, but since … well, she'd taken her company to an entirely different level thanks to the infamous club—Devotion—that they were members of.

They were what their friends called a power couple. Sometimes, due to the volume of hours they each worked during the week, Tag wasn't so sure that was meant to be a compliment. However, they did what they loved, and when they weren't working, they were spending their time together. He couldn't ask for much more than that.

But at this point in time, McKenna was definitely married to her job. Which was why he'd known she wouldn't be happy that he was taking her away for a week, but honestly, he hadn't had any other choice.

And this … this trip they were taking... Well, the timing wasn't the only surprise he had in store for her. Not that he was going to tell her that just yet. He was a smart man, after all.

"Really, Tag?" McKenna asked incredulously, her pitch rising with every word she spoke. "I just walked in the door. And now I'm supposed to pack? Where are we going?"

"I'm not tellin' you."

As he expected, her hands flew to her hips, she pursed her lips, cocked her head, and stared him down. He didn't budge. She would have to do a lot better than that to shake him up.

"So what am I supposed to pack? If I don't know where we're going, then—"

"All taken care of," he said softly, interrupting what would've likely been a long, drawn-out argument.

Sometimes he wondered how she wasn't a lawyer, as much of an argument as she liked to make. Considering he *was* a lawyer, he knew quite a few evasive maneuvers, and maybe that was why they worked so well together.

"Tag."

What should've been one syllable turned into several, and he couldn't resist any longer. Tag grinned as he stalked her, effectively backing her against the bedroom door. Curling his finger beneath her chin, he tilted her head slightly, staring down into those exotic blue-green eyes that he'd found himself lost in a million times since the day he'd met her.

"Do you trust me, McKenna?" he asked, his voice low, serious.

Her eyes widened, her mouth slowly closed, and she nodded her head.

"Good. Then leave everything up to me. The only thing I want you to do is relax. I'm gonna spend the next seven days takin' care of *you*." He punctuated his statement by tapping her lightly on the nose and smiling.

"But ... seven days! Are you serious? Really?"

Tag gently laid his finger over her lips and shook his head. "No arguing with me this time. You're not gonna win."

"Can I at least take my laptop with me?" she mumbled against his finger.

"Nope."

Aw, hell. That mischievous gleam he'd grown accustomed to ignited in her eyes, and the hint of a smile curled her lips. He dropped his hand to his side, waiting for what came next.

"What if I try to persuade you?"

He smiled. He'd been expecting this.

Tag sucked in a breath when McKenna's hand grazed his cock. The thin layer of his slacks did little to protect him from her probing fingers, and the pleasure was nearly too much.

"And how do you intend to do that?" Hell. If she wanted to play this game, he was more than happy to oblige.

"How 'bout I show you?"

His mouth went dry the instant McKenna lowered herself to her knees in front of him. She didn't hesitate before deftly unhooking his belt, releasing the button, and lowering the zipper of his slacks, freeing his cock. Nor did she waste any time before she sucked the head of his dick into the furnace of her mouth, drawing a hiss from him.

"Fuck." With one hand planted firmly on the wall, the other sliding into the silky strands of her fiery red hair, Tag gave himself over to her.

The woman had a wicked mouth. He'd learned that early on in their relationship, and for the past two years, he'd been blessed to experience it on a very regular basis.

"Damn, darlin'," he growled. "Makes me wanna fuck your mouth hard and fast."

McKenna moaned, the vibrations shooting up his shaft and detonating in his balls, a flash fire exploding in his veins.

"You want that? You want me to fuck your mouth?"

She nodded.

"Or would you prefer I tie you to the bed and spend the next half hour eating your sweet pussy while you scream my name?"

Another moan, more vibrations.

Lord have mercy. Hallelujah.

As much as he wanted to let go, to lose himself right then and there, he had an agenda. One that he needed to follow to the letter if he intended to pull this off. Succumbing to her wicked torment was a surefire way of blowing it all—no pun intended—before he got what he wanted.

And yes, there was something Tag wanted from this woman. Something he'd wanted for so long now he forgot what it was like before the need had begun clawing at his insides.

"Baby. Fuck..." Tag knew he needed to pull out of her mouth, turn the tables on her, and take control, but he was having a hard time making his brain function. His ability to reason was quite literally being sucked right out of him.

McKenna opted to add to his torture by kneading his balls with her soft, cool fingers, and he knew what she was doing. Which was why he had to put a stop to it.

"Nuh-uh. Hands down. Behind your back," he demanded, his voice rough from the pleasure coursing through him.

Her hands instantly fell to her lap, and then she tucked them behind her back, which didn't diminish his desire at all. Seeing her so submissive, doing exactly as he instructed, made his dick throb against her lips. It didn't matter that she was still wearing her work clothes—a silky turquoise blouse and a pair of sexy gray slacks that showcased her narrow hips and enticing ass. In fact, that was probably even sexier than if she'd been naked on her knees with his dick in her mouth.

Control. He had to take control.

Placing his other hand in her hair, he cradled her head and held her still while he pumped his hips forward in a slow, rhythmic pattern, driving his cock deeper.

"Don't move," he told her as he leisurely fucked her mouth. "Damn, that's good, darlin'. Suck harder." When the suction intensified, he picked up the pace, his eyes locked on her face, gauging just how much she could take. "I love your mouth. Love watching you on your knees, takin' my dick. So fuckin' hot, McKenna."

Tag was quickly approaching the point of no return, but he couldn't seem to stop. As he'd told her, she was so fucking hot, and even though he knew exactly what she was doing, tempting him until he lost every ounce of his control, he couldn't bring himself to care.

"Last chance," he warned her. "You want me to come in your mouth?"

McKenna gave him a slight nod and hummed an affirmative, which was exactly what he needed. Gripping her hair tighter, he increased his pace, fucking past her lips while she kept her eyes locked with his. A few more thrusts... "Fuck. Damn. Take it, McKenna. Swallow for me, baby."

His entire body stilled, his release barreling through him, his cock pulsing once, twice, and then he was coming in her mouth, watching as she swallowed every drop.

Sliding his dick from between her lips, he released her hair and helped her to her feet, still maintaining eye contact. When she was standing before him, a smile on her lips, he smiled back.

"You know what happens to bad girls, don't you?"

McKenna trembled slightly, but her smile never faltered, and that mischievous gleam in her eyes intensified.

"Of course you do. And for the next seven days," he said, leaning down until his mouth was close to her ear, "I fully intend to pay you back for that little stunt." He nipped her earlobe. "Do you think you can handle that?"

McKenna's arms came up, sliding around his neck, and Tag returned to his full height, looking down on her, his hands moving to her sides, his thumbs purposely grazing the sides of her breasts.

"I know I can," she stated with a full-fledged grin. "And I look forward to it."

Tag laughed and swatted her on the ass. "Of course you do."

McKenna watched as Tag strolled into their bedroom and proceeded to undress, the same as he normally did every single day when he got home from work. Granted, there had only been a few times when she'd jumped him before he had the chance to change, but in her defense, he was just too damn sexy. Sometimes she couldn't help herself.

He opened his closet door, then took a step back. First went the tie, then the expensive jacket, followed by the cuff links. And so on and so forth until he was standing in his underwear—a pair of sexy black boxer briefs that she'd bought him for Valentine's Day this year—looking like a super model. Only her sexy man was covered in ink, which merely made him that much hotter. Amplified by the fact that most people had no idea he had any ink whatsoever. Due to his very public image and his high-powered job as a corporate lawyer, he had thought ahead, only inking spots that weren't seen when he was wearing the fancy suits he preferred.

"So what time do we have to be at the airport?" she questioned, hoping to get some details out of him while she continued to ogle his delectable body. Apparently her wicked ways hadn't worked for her this time, but she knew that'd been a gamble. One she would gladly try again and again.

Men liked blow jobs; McKenna knew that. And Tag *loved* blow jobs, but he also knew that she loved giving them. To him, anyway. She didn't even expect anything in return, but she knew that didn't matter because before the night was over, or perhaps tomorrow, he would have made her come at least a dozen times. That was what he did. And she loved him for it.

In fact, she loved him for a million other reasons as well.

But she wasn't all that fond of surprises. Especially not ones that would take her away from work without giving her the opportunity to tie up any loose ends. No, it wouldn't really matter, because her office staff would definitely be able to carry her weight while she was gone—they'd done it a million times before—but McKenna simply wasn't built that way.

And Tag knew that.

Which was why she figured he was doing this. Whatever *this* was.

Granted, his revelation was rather exciting. A surprise getaway. She had absolutely no idea where they were going, or even when they would leave. Heck, she didn't even know what was packed in her suitcase, but the one thing she knew for certain—she could trust Tag to take care of her. He'd been doing it for the past two years, and he hadn't failed her. Not one single time.

Figuring she wasn't going to get much out of him now, she headed for her closet. Once she was changed into a pair of silk pajama pants and a thin tank top—after all, she wasn't finished trying to persuade him just yet—McKenna headed to the kitchen to make dinner. They alternated cooking when they didn't grab takeout, and tonight was her night.

"What do you want to eat?" she hollered, pulling open the freezer and glancing inside. A frozen four-cheese pizza, a handful of TV dinners, some sort of bagged stirfry, a bottle of vodka, ice, and a pint of Ben and Jerry's Chocolate Therapy was all that she found.

"Doesn't matter," he told her, joining her in the kitchen with his laptop in hand. The chair scraped along the wood floor as he pulled it out, his attention already on the screen in front of him.

With her hand on the freezer door, she glanced over at him. "Frozen pizza?"

"Works for me." He was now engrossed in whatever was on the laptop, which meant McKenna was on her own for a bit.

That was what they did. They worked. Day and night. Night and day.

Tag was a lawyer, which pretty much explained why he spent so much time on the phone or the computer. But he did like to have fun and often tried to persuade her to take time off and spend it with him. It wasn't that she didn't want to, and when things weren't chaotic at the office, she did take the time. That didn't mean that they hadn't fallen into the same rut as other couples who'd been together for a couple of years.

McKenna hit the buttons on the oven to preheat, then leaned against the counter and stared at the man she loved, crossing her arms over her chest. Sometimes she simply watched him, loving the various expressions he made when he was engrossed in a case, or even in simply reading an email. Tag gave one hundred and fifty percent to everything he did, and she respected the hell out of him for it.

He really was incredibly sexy. Perhaps more so now than when she'd first met him, and she remembered those initial days well. From the minute she'd laid eyes on the man, she'd been infatuated with him. And now … well, it was so much more than that.

Tag's forehead creased as he read something on the screen, worry lining the corners of his mouth. He absently ran his hand over his bald head and released a heavy breath.

And it was right then that McKenna decided to give herself over to the next seven days with him. It didn't really matter where he intended to take her; the time away would do them some good. Not to mention, she'd have him all to herself for a little while.

The oven dinged, signaling that the preheat was complete, and when Tag didn't bother to look up, McKenna smiled to herself.

Yep, she was looking forward to the next seven days. And in the meantime, she'd grab her own laptop so she could tie up a few loose ends before she disappeared with him for a week.

Chapter *Two*

The following morning, after getting up and dressed without waking McKenna, Tag spent an hour on his computer before he needed to get ready to go. After finishing up a few emails, he'd made a couple of calls, ensuring that the team of lawyers who worked for him were capable of handling anything that arose. He would be out of pocket—completely—for the first time in… Hell, it'd been a long damn time since he'd done anything that took him away from work without even a cell phone to keep him connected, but this would be worth it.

After cleaning up, loading the dishwasher with the few dishes he'd used that morning, he made two mugs of coffee and then waited until the limousine arrived before he went back to their bedroom to get McKenna. She'd never been a morning person, so getting her up early was always a gamble.

"Hey," he whispered, leaning down and nuzzling his face against her ear, kissing her neck gently. "It's time to go."

McKenna stirred, smiled, then grabbed the pillow and covered up her head. Nope, definitely not a morning person, and it seemed that not even a seven-day surprise was going to get her going first thing.

"I need you to put this on," he told her.

Well, that got her attention.

She peered out from under the pillow, her eyes sliding right to his hand, where a thin piece of dark fabric dangled from his finger.

"A blindfold?" she asked groggily.

"Yes."

"I need to get dressed," she grumbled.

"Not in the plan," he told her, leaving no room for rebuttal. "You can wear your pajamas."

"To the airport? I seriously don't think so, Tag Murphy."

He chuckled. "The limo's here. We need to go. Now quit arguing and put this on."

Without waiting for her assistance, Tag took the pillow from her, tossed it to his side of the bed, and put the blindfold over her eyes.

"Don't you dare move that," he commanded as he lifted her into his arms.

If she didn't want to get with the program, he was more than happy to take the lead.

Forty minutes later, the limo pulled into the hangar for the private jet they would be taking down to Houston, where they would then board a ship for their seven-day Caribbean cruise. She'd peppered him with questions as soon as they'd gotten in the car, but he'd managed to silence her by doing what he did best: seducing her slowly. With his mouth.

He had no intention of telling her any of his plans until they landed in Houston. For now, Tag wanted to keep her guessing. Which was exactly what she did as soon as they were buckled into the plush leather seats of the jet, awaiting takeoff. Only then did he allow her to remove the blindfold.

As soon as she could see, her eyes scanned their surroundings, likely taking note of every little detail, anything to give her a hint as to what he planned to do. That was the way her brain worked. She was a journalist, always digging for information.

"Where are we going?"

Tag peered over at her and frowned.

"Fine. Don't tell me that." She fidgeted for a moment. "Will I be able to get dressed before we land?"

"Yes," he said simply.

That earned him a small smile before McKenna turned her attention out the window.

Tag busied himself by watching her. For the next seven days, that was all he wanted to do anyway. He wanted to leave the corporate world behind them and enjoy his time with her. It'd been far too long since they'd done anything like this, although, it was safe to say they'd never done anything *exactly* like this.

"Mr. Murphy," the pilot said over the speaker. "We're ready for takeoff. Just waiting on confirmation. We'll have a total flight time of roughly sixty minutes. Clear skies all the way."

"An hour?" McKenna asked, glancing back over at him. "That doesn't leave many options."

"You're right, it doesn't," he told her with a grin. It wasn't time to share the details just yet, but he would.

Eventually.

Once the plane was in the air, Tag showed McKenna where her clothes were hanging, including her makeup bag and all the other things a woman needed. He'd had help in preparing for this trip, thankfully. If it hadn't been for Samantha and Sierra—the wives of three (yes, three) of his good friends—he likely would've found a way to disappoint McKenna from the get-go.

And he damn sure didn't intend to do that, so he'd enlisted their help.

In fact, he'd enlisted their help for the entire journey. Not only had the two women helped him to pack McKenna for the trip, they'd helped with a majority of the other preparations. And ... they would also be on board the cruise ship, along with quite a few other people—family and friends.

This trip... It was one of the most important trips of his life.

Because in the next few days, Tag was going to make McKenna his wife. And all of their family and friends were going to be along to see it.

He only hoped McKenna didn't freak out when she figured it out.

McKenna had to admit, she'd been a little nervous that Tag wasn't allowing her to do anything in preparation for this trip. But the instant she'd seen the outfit—a pair of skinny jeans, paired with a fitted emerald-green T-shirt and her favorite black blazer—not to mention, a sexy bra-and-panty set and all of her makeup and hair products, she'd relaxed exponentially.

She'd also figured that he'd had help with this setup. Not because Tag wasn't capable, but seriously, he was still a guy, and when it came to packing for a trip, men could do it in less than three minutes, and that included pulling the suitcase out from the bottom of the closet.

Well, maybe not Tag. He was one of the best-dressed men she'd ever met, and he was meticulous with his wardrobe, so she'd have to give him fifteen minutes for packing, but not much more than that.

Just as she pulled off her pajamas, ready to get dressed, a knock sounded on the small bathroom door. Knowing it could only be Tag, she unhooked the lock and allowed him to pull open the door.

He made a move to step inside and she laughed. The bathroom wasn't as small as those on a commercial flight, but it wasn't all that big, either. Barely enough room for the two of them to fit, but of course, he managed to fit inside.

"Mmm, this is exactly the way I like to see you. Maybe I shouldn't allow you to get dressed," he said warmly as he ran his finger down her collarbone and over the swell of her breast, stopping to tease her nipple.

Heat coiled inside her, making her body melt from his touch, and when he lifted her breast, bending down and sucking her into his mouth, she sighed.

"Like that?" he questioned as he teased her other breast, laving it with his tongue.

"Yes," she whispered.

"Good, then you'll love this."

McKenna wasn't sure how he managed, but Tag squatted down in front of her, lifting one of her legs up over his shoulder while he used his fingers to separate her folds. He peered up at her briefly before leaning forward and sliding his tongue along her slit, liquid fire rushing through her veins.

She gripped his head in her hands, pulling him to her as he began to lap at her pussy, delicately teasing her clit, torturing her on purpose. He loved to do that, to send her to the precipice but never send her over until he was ready. And he did that with practiced ease, continuing to devour her, licking, sucking.

"You're gonna make me come," she told him. "Make me come, Tag. *Please.* Oh, yes. Make me come."

McKenna's hands gripped the edge of the counter as she bucked her hips toward his mouth, trying to increase the friction. When he pumped two fingers inside her, his lips wrapping around her clit, his tongue flicking the sensitive bundle of nerves ruthlessly, she found herself soaring higher and higher until something inside her broke apart.

"Yes!" Her head fell back, every muscle in her body tensed, as the glorious sensation filled her, the tingle in her core erupting.

By the time she came back down from the erotic high, Tag was standing in front of her once again, cupping her face as he pressed his lips to hers. She could taste herself on his mouth, his tongue, as he kissed her hard.

She wished there was more room, enough that he could take her right there in the airplane lavatory, but she could already sense that wasn't in Tag's plan. Part of her wondered why, but she tamped down the questions.

"Now you can get dressed."

With that, he kissed her on the mouth, then disappeared, leaving her standing there, still breathing hard, wondering just what this man was up to.

It didn't take her long to get cleaned up, dressed, apply a minimal amount of makeup, and pull her hair back into a ponytail. She felt the plane begin its descent and knew she needed to get back to her seat.

Exiting the bathroom, she stuffed her clothes into a bag she found where her clothes had been hanging as Tag passed her, taking his turn going into the restroom. He was in and out before she had a chance to put away her makeup bag. Once she was finished putting everything back where she'd found it, she headed down the aisle to where Tag was waiting for her.

As the *fasten seat belt* sign flashed on, McKenna dropped into her chair just in time for the plane to land.

In Houston.

What could possibly be in Houston?

She had an idea, but in the spirit of the trip, she was trying not to think too hard. Tag wanted this to be a surprise, and she wanted to oblige him.

Which was why she donned the blindfold without him asking her to as soon as the plane was on the ground.

He helped her down the stairs, the warm May breeze tickling her face. Once they were on solid ground, he pulled her against his side and whispered in her ear. "Have I mentioned how much I like to see you blindfolded?"

"Not lately, no," McKenna replied, wondering whether or not anyone else was within earshot. Not that she really cared, but without her sight, she was left with so many questions.

Linking her fingers with Tag's, she walked alongside him. He helped her into a car—a limo, she presumed—but he didn't say much from there, other than to let her know that it'd be a thirty-minute drive.

It was a little strange for Tag to be so quiet, but McKenna didn't know what to say or do. He seemed a little nervous—why, she wasn't sure. He was always so confident, so assertive, it was endearing to see his vulnerability.

Another quality she loved so much about him.

Squeezing his fingers, she leaned closer to him. For now, she'd just relax.

Or try her hardest to, anyway.

Chapter *Three*

"We're here," Tag whispered, pressing a kiss to the top of her head.

McKenna didn't know where *here* was, but she was hoping to soon find out. Her anxiety level had ratcheted up the longer they'd sat in silence, and now, she was humming with anticipation.

Once out of the car, Tag led her only a few feet before he stopped, turning her to face him. When he pulled the blindfold off, the only thing she could see was him. Tall and broad, his big body blocked out everything else. Smiling up at him, she waited, not as patiently as she pretended, but she was doing her best.

"Do I get to know where we're going now?" she asked sweetly, keeping her voice low.

"A cruise," he told her. "Caribbean."

McKenna smiled. She'd always wanted to go on a cruise but had never gotten around to it. Her heart filled with emotion, thinking about the next seven days alone with…

"Surprise!"

McKenna's thoughts locked up at the chorus coming from behind her. It was Tag's turn to smile, but he didn't allow her to turn around.

"Just remember, I love you," he said, cupping her cheeks and chuckling. "Now take a deep breath."

McKenna allowed Tag to spin her so that she was facing the ruckus, and her heart stopped beating. A smile as wide as Texas formed on her face when she saw so many people she knew and loved. So many of her friends and family stood twenty feet away, clapping and smiling. All eyes were on her; she could feel them as she scanned the familiar faces.

Logan, Samantha, and Elijah.

Luke, Sierra, Cole, and their two-year-old daughter, Hannah.

Ashleigh, Alex, and their eighteen-month-old daughter, Riley.

Lucie, Kane, and their six-year-old daughter, Haley.

Xander and Mercedes.

She laughed when she noticed Shane Gibson and Trent Ramsey, both without dates but seemingly ready to have a good time anyway. Not that there wouldn't be women for them to flirt with on the cruise, which no doubt they would do.

Her chest swelled when she saw her parents, Jason and Diane, along with her sister, Tiffany, and brother-in-law, Matt. Due to everyone's schedules, they didn't get to spend a lot of time together, so seeing them was an unexpected surprise.

She noticed, standing off to the side, Tag's father, Jackson (that one surprised her the most), and stepmother, Victoria—Cole's mother—along with quite a few others. All there to…

"Wait," she said, turning back to face Tag. "Why are they all here?"

"To go on vacation with us."

"Really?" She wasn't buying it. Tag was the type of man who enjoyed their private time, so inviting family and friends along on a romantic getaway seemed off.

"Okay, fine," he said, cupping her face in his big, warm hands. "They're here to help us celebrate."

Celebrate? Celebrate what? Had she missed his birthday? An anniversary? McKenna was so confused.

"You've already agreed to be my wife," he told her softly, his fingers twisting the engagement ring on her left hand. "It's time to make that official."

McKenna's throat tightened, a ball of emotion threatening to choke her. This was…

"Wait. Are you saying…?" This was so much better than she'd thought. They were … getting married! "Are you serious?" she asked, wanting confirmation before she freaked out.

"Deadly," he told her, his beautiful emerald eyes scanning her face.

Throwing her arms around his neck, McKenna tried to hold back the tears of joy as she crushed her mouth to his. She'd waited for this day for so long. They'd talked about weddings, or possibly just eloping in Vegas, but they'd never gotten serious. Never taken the next step, yet here they were.

Tag chuckled, pulling his lips back from hers. "In case you're plannin' to get a little frisky there, you might wanna keep in mind that your parents are watching closely."

McKenna sobered instantly, but the smile didn't leave her lips.

Married!

Wow! She still couldn't believe it.

Okay, so the idea of a cruise was a good one.

Getting through the process ... not so much.

Thankfully, Tag had gone with the royal treatment, booking the ship's luxury rooms for him and McKenna, as well as the rest of their family and friends. It hadn't been a spur-of-the-moment decision, and it had cost a pretty penny, but luckily, he had some friends who'd gone the extra mile to help out.

It hadn't hurt that they had brought along Trent Ramsey, a very popular, very famous actor. It wasn't like Tag to name-drop, but he had to admit he'd done it. He wasn't past using his own resources to get the best for the woman he loved.

Once they were finally boarded, waiting for the ship to depart from the dock, Tag decided to steal a little alone time with McKenna before the real fun began.

The instant their private butler took his leave after going over as many details as possible in as few minutes as he could manage, Tag didn't hesitate, stalking McKenna in the oversized room that served as the living room, dining room, and kitchen.

"So what are we gonna do first?" McKenna asked melodiously, a glimmer of heat in her eyes.

"I figured I'd have dessert."

McKenna glanced around, her eyebrows downturned as she attempted to figure out what he was talking about.

"You, baby. You're my dessert."

"But, you already... On the plane."

"I didn't get my fill yet," he explained.

McKenna's face lit up as she focused her attention on him once again. Ever since her expert blow job last night, Tag had done his best to keep his hands to himself. Admittedly, he'd lost control on the plane, but he hadn't been lying when he'd told her he hadn't gotten enough of her. He wasn't sure he ever would. It wasn't easy controlling his urges considering he always wanted her. So, from the time the plane had landed, he'd been waiting for this very moment.

Tag lifted her into his arms and carried her into the bedroom. He unceremoniously tossed her onto the bed and came down atop her, crushing his lips to hers without wasting a second. He relished the taste of her, the way her tongue dueled with his so perfectly.

Her sexy moans, combined with her soft hands as they slid beneath his shirt, had Tag's body humming to life. He absolutely loved when she touched him. Loved the way her cool hands felt on his skin, the bite of pain when she dug her fingernails into his back. And he loved touching her, tasting her, making her cry out in pleasure. Hell, he was pretty sure he could get high on her.

Trailing his mouth down to her neck, he nibbled on her skin. "Take your shirt off for me."

Pushing up to give her a little room, Tag watched as McKenna pulled her T-shirt over her head, tossing it onto the floor.

"So fucking pretty." Her eyes were the same color as the Caribbean, and when she was turned on, they seemed to glow. That, along with her fiery red hair and fair skin, was a combination for the most beautiful woman in the world.

And she was his to do with as he wanted.

"Lose the bra."

Enraptured as she unhooked the front clasp, allowing the cups to fall open and reveal her full, luscious breasts and sweet, dusky nipples, Tag held himself in check. Barely.

"Now my shirt," he instructed.

She pulled his shirt up his body, then over his head, tossing it to the floor with hers. Rolling to his back, Tag pulled her with him, holding her close so he could feel her skin against his while he kissed her, hard. A desperate ache consumed him, as he fought the urge to take her roughly.

McKenna did that to him. She stirred something in him that no one had ever managed to stir before. She made his blood sizzle with her nearness.

Pulling his mouth from hers, Tag instructed her to take off her jeans, which she did with a seductive grin. As she crawled back over him, he didn't allow her to stop when she attempted to reposition herself over him, instead bringing her up until she was straddling his face, her musky scent making his head swim with need. With his hand on her hips, he jerked her closer, sliding his tongue between her slick folds, teasing her.

"Tag," McKenna cried out, her hands gripping the headboard that was attached to the wall. "Oh, yes!"

Tag didn't pause as he ate her pussy, licking, teasing, thrusting his tongue inside her as she rode his face. He could've spent a day doing that, burying his face in her cunt, fucking her with his tongue, listening to her sweet moans and cries of pleasure as her thighs squeezed his head.

"Fuck!" she screamed as her body went rigid.

Tag opened his eyes, watching her above him as she rode the waves of her orgasm. He was ready to continue to pleasure her with his mouth, but McKenna clearly had other plans. She was off the bed and trying to take off his jeans, but Tag stopped her, laughing as he got to his feet.

He undressed completely and snagged McKenna once again, lowering her to the bed, her legs dangling over the side. Easing closer to her, Tag bent his knees and guided his cock into her, watching where they were joined, sucking in a breath as he claimed her body with his. Once he was lodged in her heat, he lifted her legs, holding them against his chest as he retreated and impaled her. Hard.

"Oh, yes! Fuck me hard, Tag."

Unable to refuse her, Tag did as she requested, slamming into her as he watched her hands glide over her tits, cupping them, pinching her sweet puckered nipples while he fucked her. She was so tight, so wet, he got lost in the erotic slide of his cock inside her, the friction sending shards of electricity through him, making his balls draw up tight to his body.

"Harder!"

Tag pounded into her, gripping her legs tight to his chest. McKenna moved her hands to the edge of the mattress, holding herself still as he continued to drive into her over and over, harder, faster until she was crying out his name, her back arched, head thrown back as she came, her tight pussy milking him until he couldn't hold back.

"Damn, you're tight," he growled. "Squeeze my dick, baby. Fuck yes. Just like that." Tag's release slammed into him, his cock pulsing as he came inside her.

Without pulling out, he allowed her legs to fall open, and he leaned forward, his chest resting against her breasts, while he kept his weight from crushing her.

"I love you," he whispered, pressing his lips to hers.

"I love you, too."

"So what do you wanna do now?" he asked, pushing up onto his arms and staring down at her.

"Shower first. Maybe a little more of that," she said with a giggle. "And then we'll make an appearance for a little while. And when we get back here later, you can fulfill your promise to punish me."

"For?" he asked.

"For when I'm bad later."

Tag nodded. He was certainly on board with that plan.

God, he loved this woman.

Chapter Four

McKenna felt as though she were walking on a cloud when she emerged from the room with Tag two hours later. Her body still hummed from his delicious teasing, which he'd been relentless about when they'd showered together. He'd made her come several more times until her body was so sated, so exhausted, she'd worried she would never orgasm again.

Not that she would tell him that. Tag was always up for a challenge, and that was one he'd pursue inexorably if he thought she were serious.

"Hungry?" Tag asked as they made their way down to the main deck of the ship.

"Starving."

"Good. We've got a dinner date."

McKenna glanced up at him. She could tell by the tone of his voice that it wasn't going to be a romantic dinner between them, either. Not that she minded. In fact, she was quite eager to see her friends and family, to try to understand just what Tag had in store for her during their trip.

When they reached the dining room, McKenna took a moment to look around, awed by the sheer size. The ship was gigantic, and all of the common areas were designed for the masses. This room was no different. They could probably safely seat over a thousand people in there. The upside was that there weren't that many people there at the moment, which was why she saw a table full of faces she recognized instantly.

Tag took her hand and led her toward the group. When Sierra looked up, her face lit up like the surface of the sun.

"Yay! She's here."

That excited squeal had other heads turning, more smiles coming her way. Her father instantly got up, moving in their direction. As he had earlier, before they'd boarded the ship, he hugged her tightly. McKenna hugged him back, then went to her mother, leaning down and kissing her on the cheek.

Once the greetings were made, all the hugs and handshakes doled out, McKenna took a seat at the long table next to Mercedes, while Tag sat on her other side.

Mercedes leaned over. "This wedding business looks good on you. You're glowing."

McKenna smiled. "Not sure it's the wedding that did it, but thank you," she replied softly.

Mercedes laughed, that sexy, raspy voice of hers drawing a lot of attention. "We were beginning to wonder whether y'all would ever emerge."

Smiling at her friend, she said, "Trust me, I thought about locking him in there and having my wicked way with him again."

"If it's any consolation, we're glad you're here," Mercedes mumbled.

"I'm the one who's glad. Look at y'all. I can't believe you're here. This is amazing."

"So? Did it work? Did he surprise you?" Samantha McCoy asked instantly.

"He did," McKenna said, remembering their morning fondly. "He definitely did."

McKenna glanced around at all the faces of the people who'd helped Tag to pull this off, her heart swelling with love as she did. These were her friends and family, a group of people who'd become incredibly important to her.

In any given week, they would all try to get together at least once if their schedules meshed. Sometimes it didn't work the way they would've liked, but they had all agreed that they wouldn't allow their lives to get in the way of their friendship if they could help it.

Of course, that was easier said than done.

Samantha, a high-level executive who contracted for XTX, was an incredibly ambitious woman, as was her husband, Logan, the president of that very same company. The two of them spent as much time, if not more, than McKenna and Tag did working. So much so that they'd mutually decided that they wouldn't have time to devote to children. However, they did have time to devote to keeping the spice in their sex life, which was where Elijah Penn came in. Last year, they'd ventured into a permanent threesome with him, and based on the smile on Samantha's face, they were incredibly happy. Samantha was sitting between the two men she loved, leaning against Logan while her husband spoke to his twin brother, Luke, Luke's husband, Cole, and their wife, Sierra.

As was usually the case, the three men were fussing over Hannah—Luke, Cole, and Sierra's two-year-old daughter—who was doing her best to get down from her chair, clearly wanting to run around and not be stuck in one place. The little girl was adorable, and the men in her life were wrapped around her little finger. McKenna completely understood why. The little girl was so much like her mother and her fathers. Sweet like Sierra yet mischievous like Luke and Cole. Very cute on top of that with her dark hair and bright blue eyes.

A strange sensation gripped McKenna's insides as she realized she could be having a baby sometime in the near future. She and Tag had agreed that they wanted babies, but they knew the timing was off. Not to mention, they wanted to wait until they were married.

Which they would be very soon.

Although, McKenna realized, she didn't know when the actual date was.

"You okay?" Sierra asked, concern etched on her pretty face as she stared back at McKenna.

"Great," she said, realizing she'd been frowning, and she certainly hadn't intended to bring down the party, so she plastered on another smile.

"So, McKenna. Care to share how your man managed to pull this off? You really had no idea?" Logan asked.

"None whatsoever," McKenna said. "He kidnapped me. Blindfolded and in my pajamas."

Several people chuckled.

"He's just lucky it was a private plane," McKenna stated, smirking at Tag. "I doubt the TSA would've appreciated me being there half-dressed."

Tag leaned in and whispered, "Oh, they would've loved it."

McKenna refused to blush. The man did his best to make that happen on a frequent basis, but she'd learned to deal with him. Not to mention, she wasn't really the blushing type. After all, her world was ensconced with plenty of blush-worthy detail. She would never have made it this far if a little dirty talk reddened her fair skin all the time.

"I think it's incredibly romantic," Sam offered. "You've got yourself a keeper there."

"That I do." McKenna knew how lucky she was.

"And she's gonna make it official very soon," Tag inserted.

"How soon?" McKenna questioned, hoping someone would give her a little bit to go on.

As though they all knew she wasn't supposed to know, every mouth at the table instantly closed, words replaced by grins.

"Come on. I'm getting married. Shouldn't I know when?" Not that she really cared when. The simple fact that she would be Tag's wife was honestly enough for her.

"Truth is," Alex spoke, holding his eighteen-month-old daughter, Riley, on his lap. "He hasn't told us yet."

McKenna's gaze snapped to Tag's. "Really?"

His lips curled at the corners. "They'll know. As soon as you do."

"And that'll be?"

"When I'm ready to tell you. Now who's ready to eat?"

McKenna laughed. It was just like Tag to maintain control of everything. Then again, that was an aspect of his personality that she found incredibly hot.

So, who was she to argue?

Dinner was fantastic, but it probably could've tasted like dirt and Tag wouldn't have cared. His attention had been focused on the woman beside him, the woman he adored more than anything else.

He'd watched her chat with Samantha, Sierra, Mercedes, and Ashleigh while she ate. Although her attention always seemed to be on those four women, her hand had continued to caress his thigh, letting him know that she knew where he was at all times. That was something she'd always done, something he found endearing.

While Tag had engaged in the conversation related to Devotion—the fetish club owned by Luke and Cole, with several private investors—he'd watched the people he'd grown close to over the last two years. He considered himself blessed to have so many friends who ultimately were there to watch his back.

At one point, Tag had been involved in a threesome with Logan and Samantha, and surprisingly, their friendship had survived once Tag had taken his leave from their erotic escapades back when he'd found himself attracted to McKenna. Since then, Logan and Samantha had ventured into a much more permanent relationship with Elijah Penn. The three of them looked happy, and Tag was grateful for that.

Then there was the intimidating Xander Boone, one of the silent partners in Devotion, whose mere presence at the table did not go unnoticed. The man was massively built; six foot six inches of pure muscle. However, it wasn't merely his size that drew attention to him. He was also a Dom, and it seemed that, with very little effort, the guy garnered attention. His wife, Mercedes, was just as dominating as he was, except for when she looked at Xander. It was in those heated looks that Tag—and likely anyone who knew the couple—saw just how submissive she was to him.

Of course, there were also the kids, who seemed to steal the show. Haley, Riley, and Hannah were all three incredibly active, despite the fact that six-year-old Haley had attempted to keep Riley and Hannah entertained. Since that was easier said than done, it explained why their parents had opted to take their leave as soon as the meal was finished, leaving Tag and McKenna with Mercedes and Xander, Trent, Shane, her parents, Jason and Diane, as well as McKenna's older sister, Tiffany, and her husband, Matt. Tag's father and stepmother had cut out early, but that wasn't surprising. Despite the fact his father had come, Tag knew the man's sole focus was on his wife, but that'd always been the case.

"So, you're still not tellin' us when the big day is?" Tiffany asked.

Tag glanced over at her and grinned. "Not yet."

"Why the secret?" Matt questioned.

"No reason." Squeezing McKenna's hand beneath the table, Tag added, "I just like to keep my girl on her toes."

"Well, I'd say you accomplished that well," Jason stated. "And very impressive, I might add."

"He's good to me," McKenna said.

Truth was, McKenna was good to him, and this was merely his way of showing her just what she meant to him.

"What do you say we head over to the cigar lounge?" Xander asked, glancing over at Mercedes and McKenna. "That is, if you ladies don't mind."

"Don't mind us," Mercedes said. "We'll find some trouble to get into on our own."

"Well, I think we're going to head to the casino," Diane told them.

"I think we'll join you," Tiffany added.

Tag glanced at McKenna.

"Go. Have fun. Mercedes is right, we'll find plenty of trouble to get into."

Tag leaned in close and kissed her lips. "You do that. If I recall correctly, I'll owe you a spanking when you get back to the room tonight."

"That you will," McKenna said with a wink.

Twenty minutes later, once the rest of the group dispersed, Tag found himself in a rather impressive cigar lounge with Xander, Shane, and Trent, sitting at a small table in the back.

"Logan's on his way back down," Xander informed them. "I'll be right back."

Tag watched as Xander went to the bar and spoke to the bartender before returning. Just as Xander was sitting down, Luke and Cole arrived, filling two of the extra chairs at the table. Logan wasn't far behind.

"You do know you've set the bar really high for the rest of us, don't you?" Luke's question was directed at Tag as they each retrieved a cigar from a humidor on the table.

Tag smirked. "That was the plan. I can't let you get lazy in your old age."

"Lazy?" Cole countered. "Try chasin' after Hannah for a few hours. That'll show you just how not lazy we are."

"She's a handful," Logan added.

"That she is, but cute enough to make us overlook that," Luke muttered.

The waiter delivered drinks, setting a glass in front of each of them and disappearing again.

"When are y'all gonna have one of your own?" Logan asked Xander.

"One of these days," Xander confirmed with a wide grin. "We're definitely tryin'."

"Probably shouldn't let your wife put your balls in a cage," Shane said deadpan. "That'll help the little guys along."

Tag laughed, nearly spewing the brandy out of his nose.

"Not a visual I needed," Luke said, chuckling.

"Then don't hang out at the club," Shane added. "She's been known to chain his ass up."

"Not anymore she doesn't," Xander said.

"Sore sport," Shane told him.

"Just wait," Cole said. "It'll be your turn one of these days."

Tag studied Shane for a moment. It wasn't a secret that the man had a thing for Xander's assistant, a cute girl who, if Tag had to guess, wouldn't last a minute in that Dom's world.

"Not if I can help it," Shane answered. "Maybe we should look to this one." Shane nodded toward Trent. "He's more likely to get swept up in the romance before I am."

Trent shook his head. "I'm havin' too much fun to settle down."

Everyone knew that Trent Ramsey, famous movie star, was a playboy. He definitely had a fascination for women, but he had yet to settle down. He was the youngest of the group, and according to him, his career aspirations hadn't yet been met, although he'd ventured further from acting over the last year. He was being incredibly picky about the roles he played, spending most of his time driving up revenues for Devotion and trying to come up with a plan to conquer the world.

"You heard from any of the Walker boys lately?" Trent asked, clearly attempting to deflect the attention.

Xander was the one to speak up. "Mercedes and I are headin' down there to help them work on some things. They're putting more focus on BDSM for the summer months, and Mercedes has made it her mission to ensure they're doin' it right."

"Travis wanted to be here," Luke inserted. "But he's focused on his family at the moment."

Tag knew that Travis Walker had recently had a baby with his husband and wife. Tag hadn't talked to him in quite some time because the man's trips up to Dallas were less frequent now that he was a family man. Not that Tag blamed the guy.

"So, how long after you tie the knot before you have kids?" Shane asked Tag.

Scanning the faces before him, he puffed on the cigar before answering. "As soon as fucking possible," he told them honestly.

"How long have y'all been together?" Trent asked.

"Two years."

"Damn, has it been that long?" Xander asked. "Time flies when you're havin' fun."

No doubt about that, Tag thought to himself.

Chapter *Five*

Friday morning

"Good mornin'," Tag greeted McKenna when she joined him out on their private deck the following morning.

He'd woken up early, snuck out of their room, and decided to get some fresh air. He'd been out there for nearly two hours, enjoying the endless miles of beautiful blue water while drinking coffee and thinking about all that they'd done in the few days they'd been at sea. Well, he'd been trying to think about those things but mostly found himself wondering about the details of the wedding. Sierra had assured him that he had nothing to worry about, that she was managing everything with the coordinator on the ship, but it wasn't easy for Tag to leave something so crucial up to someone else.

However, aside from the chaotic thoughts running through his head—all regarding details for the wedding that was in the process of being set up—he'd enjoyed a little time to himself.

But now that McKenna was there, he felt much more at peace.

She stepped out onto the deck, his eyes trailing to her long, sexy legs.

"Come here," he said, motioning with his hand for her to come join him on his lounge chair.

McKenna padded over to him, took his hand, and allowed him to pull her down on top of him. She was wearing one of his T-shirts, and as he slid his hand up her thigh, inching beneath the cotton, he realized she wasn't wearing anything else.

"Mmm," he mumbled.

"You like that?" she asked with a hint of amusement.

"I do." After kissing her forehead, Tag pressed his cheek to her head as he ran his fingers over the smooth skin of her thigh, his eyes once again scanning the clear blue horizon.

"So what's the plan for today?" McKenna mumbled.

"Not sure yet." They'd spent the last two days enjoying all the amenities that the ship had to offer, including spending last night at the casino, where McKenna had made a killing playing craps. She'd done so well she'd drawn the attention of quite a few people, including Tag. He hadn't done so well, but his heart hadn't been in the gambling because he'd been so taken aback by how incredible McKenna was.

Sometimes he wondered whether or not he'd turned into a sap over the years. Or maybe, this was what a relationship was supposed to be like. Especially one when you found yourself in love with your best friend. And that's what McKenna was to him. His best friend. His lover.

The woman he wanted to spend the rest of his life with.

McKenna reached for his hand, which was still skimming her thigh. She pulled his arm, encouraging him to move closer to the warmth between her legs.

"You want me to tease you?" he mumbled.

"Mmm hmm."

Unable to resist, Tag eased his hand between her legs, helping her to shift so that she was still situated on his lap but so that he could slide his finger through her folds.

"You're wet."

"I was thinking about you," she told him.

"That so? What were you thinking about?" Tag pushed his finger inside her, gently fucking her.

McKenna moaned.

"Tell me. Tell me what you were thinkin' about."

"All the dirty things you do to me," she admitted.

"Elaborate," he told her, stilling his finger as he waited for her to respond.

McKenna squirmed, but Tag refused to indulge her until she answered.

"I was lying in bed, alone, touching myself and thinking about your fingers, your mouth…"

Tag grinned. "That's not enough and you know it. What about them?"

He wanted her to share the details with him, to give him a play by play of all the things she wanted him to do to her. He'd do them, there was no doubt about it, but he loved hearing her say them.

"I prefer you to tell me," she whispered. "I love hearing what you'll do to me, as you do them."

Of course she did.

"Like when I thrust my finger into your wet pussy?" he asked, his actions following his words.

McKenna's inner muscles clamped down on his finger as she moaned, spreading her legs wider, giving him better access.

"Or how about when I thrust two fingers into you?"

Tag added another finger, pumping them into her slow and easy.

"Yes. Oh, God, yes."

"Take off the shirt," he ordered.

McKenna sat up, dislodging Tag's fingers from inside her. She whipped the shirt off over her head, tossing it to the deck floor.

"Now stand up."

When she got to her feet, he followed her. Taking her hand, he led her back through their cabin and out onto the other secluded deck, which had a hot tub. The sun was beating down on them, so it was a good thing he hadn't heated the water. That was the last thing he needed, something else to heat him up. McKenna was doing a damn fine job of that all on her own, simply by breathing.

Helping McKenna into the tub, he kept her from going all the way in, insisting that she sit on the edge while he rid himself of his boxers, and then joined her.

"Have I mentioned how much I love seeing you naked?" McKenna asked, her heated gaze traveling over him as he climbed into the water.

"You might've mentioned it a time or two."

"Well, I do. A lot."

Gripping his cock in his fist, Tag pumped himself a couple of times, his eyes perusing McKenna's lovely body.

"And I especially enjoy watching you jack off," she said, her voice raspy.

"Is that right?"

"Yes."

"And that's what you want me to do now?" he asked, continuing to stroke his cock while she remained riveted to his hand leisurely gliding up and down.

McKenna nodded.

He allowed her to watch him for a few minutes, his cock thickening in his fist, the heat of her gaze making his balls ache with the need to be inside her. He had no desire to come in his own hand, not when she was within arm's reach, though.

"Why'd you stop?" she asked, her eyes lifting to meet his when he allowed his hand to fall into the water at his side.

He moved closer to her, situating himself between her thighs. "Now, I'm more interested in making you come. And I plan to do that by telling you all the wicked things I'm going to do to you."

McKenna's body had begun to hum with arousal as she sat on the edge of the hot tub watching Tag stroke himself, the muscles on his arms and chest flexing deliciously. He truly was the sexiest man she'd ever seen.

Watching him, admiring every inch of him, was such a turn on, especially when he was pleasuring himself. He didn't do it often, at least not when she was watching, but she knew he preferred to make her the center of his attention.

She couldn't complain, either, because the man was incredibly skilled in that department. And she loved the way he spoke to her. The dirty talk, the promises of what he would do to her... It'd always driven her wild. Now was no exception.

"Open yourself for me," Tag instructed as he eased onto the seat between her spread legs.

A chill raced down McKenna's spine at his forceful words. She loved when he became domineering and persistent. He was so damn... What was the word? Alpha? Yeah. That was probably the one she was looking for. It made her entire body tingle.

McKenna slid her hand down between her thighs, her fingers separating her folds while she watched Tag's eyes widen as he stared at her most intimate place.

"I need to taste you," he muttered, his head moving closer.

Keeping her eyes locked between her legs, McKenna watched as his lips brushed over her stomach, working lower until his warm breath caressed her mound. His eyes lifted to hers once more just as his fingers parted her folds, his tongue darting out, brutally swiping over her sensitive clit, causing her body to jerk in response.

Tag's arms pushed her thighs wider, holding her open while he proceeded to drive her crazy with his tongue, flicking her clit, thrusting into her. He continued the exquisite torment while her body throbbed with pleasure. He was going to make her come right there, sitting on the edge of the hot tub.

Although their outdoor space was private, she still wondered whether someone could see what they were doing. Considering they were on the top floor, there weren't any cabins above that overlooked theirs, but that didn't mean there weren't cameras somewhere taking in all the action.

Not that she cared. Not with Tag's tongue sending shards of electricity across every nerve ending.

Gripping Tag's smooth head in her hands, McKenna pulled him closer, intensifying the friction as he pushed her closer and closer to the edge of orgasm, rushing toward the pinnacle of pleasure.

"Tag," she moaned, unable to hold on, although she never wanted it to end. "Oh! Yes!"

McKenna pushed her hips forward, pulling his head closer, increasing the friction of his tongue against her clit. Grinding against him, she closed her eyes. "Tag!"

As her body skyrocketed into bliss, Tag pulled her into the water before the waves had ceased, impaling her on his cock and sending a surge of pleasure slamming into her.

"Ride me, baby," he ordered, gripping her hips as she faced him.

McKenna didn't hesitate, lifting and dropping onto him, taking the full brunt of his penetration to the deepest part of her, the friction so intoxicating she knew she was going to come again.

But before that could happen, Tag stopped her by digging his fingertips into her hips. "Turn around."

He forced her to stand, turning her so that she faced away from him as he filled her quickly. His body surrounded her as he held her tightly to him. McKenna gripped the far side of the tub, bending at the waist as he fucked her hard and fast, one of his arms wrapped tightly around her waist, his breath warm against her neck.

"I love being inside you," he told her. "Love filling you, feeling your cunt grip my dick."

McKenna tightened her inner muscles, squeezing him until he moaned.

"Just. Like. That." He punctuated his words with violent thrusts of his hips until McKenna was no longer holding back, she was soaring once more, another orgasm rocking her.

"God yes, baby. Come. Come all over my cock."

Tag let out a deep, gravelly roar as he came, his hips slamming into her ass as he filled her. Once they both settled, Tag pulled out of her, then situated her onto his lap in the water, his arms wrapped tightly around her.

"I heard you're goin' out with the girls tonight."

McKenna kissed his neck, cuddling up to him. "That's the rumor. What about you? What will y'all be doing?"

"No idea, but I've been told it's guys' night. The nanny will watch the kids while we all enjoy a night out."

"The girls are so cute," McKenna muttered. "But they're a handful. Not sure how their parents manage to keep up with them."

"One day, that'll be us," Tag said.

A ribbon of warmth trickled through McKenna's chest at the thought of having babies with Tag. They'd talked about it, but she knew they'd been putting it off. Not only because they wanted to wait until they were married but also because of their careers. However, they both completely agreed they'd be able to do both—have careers and babies.

Now, as she sat in the warmth of Tag's arms, waiting patiently for the moment when she got to say I do to this man, McKenna let the euphoric feeling wash over her. She loved him. With everything that she was.

And now … they were about to embark on the rest of their lives together.

Chapter *Six*

"You win," Luke said to Cole when Tag approached.

"That I do," Cole agreed, grinning at Tag.

"What the hell did y'all bet on now?" Tag asked, not sure he wanted to know.

"Whether or not you'd look like a lawyer when you got here," Cole answered.

"And what did you win?" Tag questioned. "Wait. Don't answer that. I don't wanna know."

The mischievous smirk on Luke's mouth said it all. If Tag had to guess, Luke and Cole would be hidden away in some dark corner—only because this was a family cruise and not their own private fetish club where they could get down and dirty in public—sometime in the foreseeable future.

"Smart man," Luke stated.

When the bartender made his way down to their end of the bar, Tag ordered a scotch.

"Xander's over at the blackjack table with McKenna's father and brother-in-law," Cole informed him. "Alex, Kane, Trent, and Shane are dumping money at the craps table. Logan and Eli aren't here yet."

Tag glanced around, wondering where his father was. He was the only person that Cole didn't mention, not that Tag was all that surprised. It seemed that these last few days, Jackson had been using this trip as his personal vacation. After the first dinner they'd all shared together, Jackson and Victoria had spent most of their time alone.

That only bothered Tag somewhat. The fact that his father had agreed to join them on the trip at all was shocking. The man spent his days worshipping his wife, not worried about anyone other than her. He could've asked Cole if he'd seen his mother, but Tag's stepbrother looked otherwise occupied as he stared at Luke with a knowing smirk on his lips.

Before Tag had met McKenna, he'd allowed his father's behavior to get to him. He had spent the majority of his life playing second fiddle to first, his own mother, and then to Victoria when Jackson had remarried after Tag's mother's death.

Tag could somewhat understand at this point in his life because he was infatuated with McKenna, wanted to spend every waking moment with her. Even now, after two years of being with her. But he still couldn't imagine putting everyone and everything on the back burner. Certainly not the children he intended to have with McKenna.

"Get outta your head," Luke commanded. "We're here to have a good time tonight."

Tag glanced over at Luke and nodded. "You're right. Did you tell Sierra that they'd be staying with McKenna tonight?" Tag asked.

"I did," Luke confirmed. "It took both of us to get her to calm down."

Tag shook his head and laughed. "I wouldn't doubt it."

"What?" Cole asked, looking sheepish. "She's a handful. Sometimes—"

"Don't finish that sentence," Tag said with a chuckle.

"Seriously, though, they're all excited about the wedding. So, of course, when I told her that tonight's McKenna's bachelorette party, Sierra got on the phone."

"With who?" Tag asked.

"Guest services."

"About?"

"She wanted to see if they had male strippers on board."

"Oh, Lord," Tag said on a sigh.

"Good news," Cole inserted. "They didn't."

"Bad news," Luke added. "We volunteered to be the strippers."

" *We* who?" Tag exclaimed, turning to face two of his closest friends, one of whom just happened to be his stepbrother.

"Well, after her parents go back to their cabin, and yours, if they join us tonight, we'll be putting on a show for the ladies," Luke explained.

"Are you fucking serious?" Tag questioned, praying that their somber expressions were part of the joke.

"They're very serious," said a voice from behind him.

Tag turned to see Logan approach, Elijah walking alongside him. "We're apparently the entertainment for the night."

"Oh, hell."

"They were very accommodating, offering up one of the clubs for tonight's performance." Elijah smirked.

"I hope y'all don't plan for me to strip," Tag said, downing the scotch the bartender had just delivered before signaling for another.

"Oh, your name's definitely on the roster."

"Xander agreed to go first," Logan stated with a laugh.

Tag's gaze scanned the room, looking for the giant Dom.

"It's not like we're not used to gettin' naked in public," Cole countered.

"Y'all, sure," Tag agreed. "Me, not so much." Although Tag was a member of Devotion, and yes, on occasion he had been known to enjoy the public exhibition that the club afforded them, it was rare.

Regardless, stripping for a group of rowdy women was an entirely different story.

"Just think, maybe you'll make a few bucks out of the deal," Luke said.

Tag glared at his friends, wondering what they hell they'd been thinking when they'd decided this was a good idea.

But more importantly, he wanted to know when the hell Luke McCoy had become the optimist.

"You should have something stronger than that," Sam told McKenna when she joined them at the table. "It's your last night as a single woman."

McKenna chuckled. "I haven't been single for a long time."

"Touché," Sam stated. "But tomorrow's the official day."

There was no way for McKenna to hide the huge grin that split her face. She'd come down to join Sierra and Ashleigh at the ship's outdoor bar an hour ago. She hadn't been there for two minutes when Sierra's excitement had gotten the best of her, and McKenna's friend had blurted that tonight was the official bachelorette party and tomorrow would be her wedding day.

From that moment onward, McKenna's nerves had been frayed, her excitement palpable. She'd also given considerable thought to what a night of boozing would do to her, which was why she intended to play it safe, stick with wine.

"I assume we're gonna do something a little more exciting than this tonight," Mercedes said as she pulled out a chair and took a seat beside McKenna.

"Oh, we are," Sierra stated with a smirk.

McKenna glanced over at her friend, studying her face. Sierra was terrible at keeping secrets.

"Go ahead. Tell them," Sam said, a matching grin on her face.

"We got us some male strippers," Sierra said excitedly.

McKenna's eyebrows lifted. "On this ship? They have male strippers?"

"No," Sierra said quickly. "But tonight they do."

"What does that mean?" Ashleigh questioned, looking just as curious as McKenna was.

Sierra leaned in as though she were about to tell a national security secret. "The boys are gonna be the strippers."

"Are..." McKenna couldn't get the question out because she started to laugh, imagining all of their men working it up on stage.

"Think *Magic Mike*, only ... hotter," Sierra added.

McKenna wasn't sure that was possible. "You mean..."

"Yep," Sierra confirmed. "Luke, Cole, Logan, Tag, Kane, Xander, Shane, Trent, *and* Alex are gonna strut their stuff for us tonight."

Glancing around the table at all of her friends, McKenna's grin widened. "And they agreed to this?"

"Everyone except Tag, but that's because it was a surprise," Sam informed them.

"Xander even volunteered to go first," Mercedes announced. "Can you imagine?"

"Does he even have any rhythm?" Lucie asked Mercedes. "I can tell you that Kane doesn't possess an ounce of it."

"Not a lick," Mercedes admitted with a chuckle. "But I can guarantee I'll have my dollar bills ready."

"Kane really agreed to this?" McKenna asked Lucie.

"I haven't talked to him. But he's always been a team player," Lucie admitted.

Lucie's husband, Kane, managed Club Destiny, the nightclub that'd originally been the front for the fetish club before Luke closed down The Club at Club Destiny and reopened it as Devotion. McKenna didn't see much of Lucie and Kane. They spent their time working or with their daughter, Haley. From what Tag had said, the couple was trying for another baby, but as of yet, they hadn't gotten pregnant.

"So when do the festivities begin?" Ashleigh asked.

"We're waiting for McKenna's parents to go to bed. We asked Tiffany if she and Matt wanted to join in, but she politely declined."

McKenna was grateful for that. It would've been a little awkward to see her straight-laced brother-in-law stripping for a room full of women. Not to mention, Tiffany was a jealous woman, and McKenna doubted her sister would've been able to sit back and take all the women cheering him on.

"What about Tag's parents?" Ashleigh asked.

"They're here somewhere, but they didn't commit to joining us tonight," Sierra explained.

McKenna's gut tightened at the thought of Jackson not wanting to spend time with his son. After all, Tag had been the one to extend the olive branch, inviting his father when he would've preferred to leave him back on dry land. Their relationship hadn't improved over the years, neither of them putting forth much effort. Although McKenna never understood how a father could be so blind to his own children, she didn't push the issue. She'd had plenty she wanted to say to the man, but for Tag's sake, she'd always kept her mouth shut.

"Well, I can't wait," Mercedes said. "It'll be interesting. Especially if Luke actually does follow through."

Sierra grinned. "Oh, he'll be up there. I promise."

The twinkle in the other woman's eyes spoke of secrets that McKenna didn't even want to know about. That threesome never ceased to amaze her. Luke was opening up, and McKenna knew that all of the thanks went to both Sierra and Cole. It was incredible what love could do to a person.

It seemed as though it could even get an uptight man to strip on stage.

But as entertaining as she knew that would be, McKenna was most interested in seeing her own man up there. Because no matter what these other women said, Tag would definitely steal the show.

Chapter Seven

"I can't believe y'all are really gonna make me do this," Tag told Luke and Cole as they led the way down a long, narrow hallway to the area behind the stage in the nightclub that had been sanctioned off to them for the night.

"I told you to have another drink," Cole said, glancing back at Tag over his shoulder.

"I could've had ten more. It wouldn't have made me agree to this," Tag informed his so-called friends.

Xander's giant hand landed on Tag's back. "How hard could it be? Just get up there, rip off your shirt, make the ladies go crazy. Simple as that."

"I thought—" Trent was instantly silenced by Xander.

Tag stopped, causing the others behind him to stop abruptly. "What's goin' on?"

"Nothin'," Luke stated. "Come on. We've got a show to put on."

Something was off. Tag could feel it. Luke McCoy was a lot of things, but eager to strip for a room full of women wasn't one of them.

Luke opened a door and took a step back, allowing Tag and the others to enter. The area was dark, with only a few dim lights from above providing enough light to see where they were going and that was about it.

"Dressing rooms are over there," Cole pointed out.

"Based on what you've told me," Tag stated gruffly, "we aren't going to need them. No need to dress if you're just gonna take it all off."

A sharp knock sounded on the door behind them, and Tag turned with the others to see who was there.

"Gentlemen," the younger man said as he stuck his head in the door. "I'm here to set up the sound system and show you how to work it. I've also brought the music you requested."

"And what song are we strippin' to?" Tag questioned, not really wanting to know the answer to that.

Cole smirked. "Have you seen *Magic Mike*?"

"No," Tag stated firmly. "No intention of seein' it, either."

"Well, then the song'll just be a surprise," Xander added.

"Nope. He's gotta watch it. Come on," Logan commanded, turning toward the dressing rooms.

Tag obediently followed Logan and the others into the dressing room. What he saw before him made his mouth go dry.

"What the hell are those?"

"Costumes," Shane informed him, amusement in his steady gaze.

Hanging on the wall in front of them were—Tag paused to count—ten outfits. Several of them were black sweat pants and white hoodies, while the rest were the opposite—white sweatpants with black hoodies.

"Good news," Elijah stated. "No G-strings."

A few chuckles sounded behind him. That's when he noticed there were black boxer briefs along with shoes for each of the outfits.

Holy shit.

They'd planned this well in advance obviously, because upon inspection, Tag noticed that, yes, they were all appropriately sized, and he doubted it was a coincidence that they'd find the exact sizes at the ship's gift shop.

Trent appeared in front of him holding an iPad. "Watch this."

With the push of a button, a video appeared on the screen. Tag could only assume it was the scene from the movie they had referenced.

"Fuck," Tag groaned. "Seriously. Y'all expect me to do *that*?"

"No, we expect you to follow our lead. Your goal is to dance for your woman," Cole informed him. "That's all you have to do. Focus on McKenna."

Tag figured he might be able to do that, but as far as the moves… Well, he had none.

The video continued to play, and Tag found himself laughing hysterically. He could imagine Luke, Cole, Logan, Xander, Kane, Alex, Elijah, Shane, and Trent performing to this song. But he absolutely could not picture himself doing it. He'd look like a fucking dancing monkey.

Fuck.

"All right. Who's ready to get this show on the road?" Xander boasted with a deep, rumbling chuckle. "Time to change."

From that moment forward, Tag was ushered where the others wanted him to go. He managed to change into the black sweatpants and white hoodie, along with a pair of white shoes that he would never in his life have purchased for himself. He tried to ignore the anxiety that erupted in his gut.

Focus on McKenna.

Yes, that was certainly the plan.

Once everyone was dressed, they made their way back to the stage. It was no longer dark, but lit up with red lights from behind the curtain. No one was there yet, which Tag considered a good thing. He wasn't even close to being comfortable with this.

The others were laughing and joking, although Tag didn't find anything funny about having to get up on stage and do a strip tease for his future bride and her crazy friends. *His* crazy friends.

Heaven help him, this was not going to go well.

Speaking of friends... From the other side of the curtain that blocked off the backstage area, an eruption of giggles and cheers sounded, signaling the arrival of their audience.

"Y'all do know that I'll be payin' you back for this. In the very near future," Tag grumbled.

"Oh, we know," Luke said. "Lighten up a bit."

"Someone wanna tell me what Luke's drinkin'? Since when did he volunteer to strip for women?"

"You only live once," Luke assured him.

Tag simply stared at the other man's back as he retreated, heading toward the stage.

"Trent, you're up," Cole announced.

"I thought Xander was goin' first," Tag asked, confused.

"He is, but we'll let the actor get up there and set it up."

Great.

Just fucking great.

Tag peered around the curtain, scanning the room to see the women who'd be watching them. McKenna had a front-row seat, and the others were spread out around her. The tables had been left where they were stored, and only chairs sat in front of the stage, likely to give them more room to dance.

Right.

Like Tag knew how to fucking dance.

"You're not nervous, are you?" Kane questioned, coming to stand beside him.

"You're *not*?" Tag retorted.

"Like Luke said, you only live once."

Right. You only live once.

And then you die of humiliation.

McKenna was unable to hide her excitement. For the last hour, she'd shared a couple of drinks with her friends, laughed at their stories, and ultimately anticipated what the night would bring, still a little shocked.

The boys were going to strip.

Even the thought made her giggle as she sat at the front of the group, her chair in the center, facing the stage. The black curtains were backlit with red lighting, giving the entire area a sexy, seductive feel.

"You ready for this?" Mercedes called out from behind her.

"Absolutely," McKenna confirmed. She was more than ready.

Her attention was drawn to the side of the stage as Trent Ramsey, the incredibly handsome and equally famous actor came waltzing out with a huge grin plastered on his face.

"Ladies," he greeted.

A round of catcalls sounded from behind her, and McKenna laughed.

"Are y'all ready for this?"

More yelling and cheers made McKenna's grin spread across her face. A tingle of anticipation started in her belly and worked its way throughout her body.

"Remember, no touching," Trent said with a smirk.

Right. Like they weren't going to touch.

He disappeared as fast as he'd come. There was movement behind the black curtain, but it was evident there were bodies lining up. Big bodies.

Unable to help herself, McKenna clapped with the others.

The lights went off, pitching the entire room into complete darkness. Although McKenna was close to the stage, she couldn't see anything.

And then it started.

"Pony" by Ginuwine started playing, causing her belly to tighten with anticipation, and the red lights near the curtains began flashing, matching the familiar beat.

"Take it all off!" Sam yelled, making the rest of them laugh.

Xander appeared, all six and a half feet of him. He was wearing white sweatpants and a black hoodie, along with a ball cap. That's when McKenna realized they were mimicking the scene from *Magic Mike*—one of her favorites.

"Woohoo!" Mercedes yelled when her man moved forward, his dance moves surprisingly good. He managed to keep the beat, but then McKenna's eyes were drawn to the others—all nine of them—as they moved onto the stage, their moves fairly choreographed.

Well, all except for Tag, who looked as though he might turn tail and run, which made McKenna smile. She was so proud of him. She knew this wasn't easy, but there he was, giving it his all.

The excitement level rose. A deafening roar erupted in the room as the women around her went a little crazy.

Ten big, sexy men unzipped their hoodies, ripped them from their arms, and tossed them to the side, leaving them shirtless and...

Holy hell.

She scanned all of the sexy torsos, but when she fixed her eyes on Tag, McKenna couldn't look away. Their gazes slammed into one another as he moved forward. Gone was the initial fear she'd seen, and in its place something much, much … sexier.

He was focused only on her, and who would've thought that Tag Murphy could dance so well, but holy shit, he had some serious moves.

The song continued to play as the men moved down from the stage, into the audience. When Tag was directly in front of her, McKenna's breaths rushed in and out of her lungs. She didn't move, didn't reach for him, but damn, she wanted to.

We're gonna get nasty, baby.

The words echoed in the room, followed by more cheering, and that was when Tag straddled her lap, his hips gliding forward and back in a sensual move that nearly knocked McKenna from her seat. She had no idea how long he continued to give her the hottest lap dance imaginable, but then he moved back, as did the others.

They backed up closer to the stage, turning away from them as they kicked off their shoes. Their hands went to the waistband of their sweats and then…

"Fuck yes! Take it off!"

McKenna laughed, her eyes glued to Tag's extremely fine backside. Her eyes raked over the tattoos that covered his smooth skin. And when he was clad in only a pair of black boxer briefs, which, sadly, he didn't take off, she couldn't contain herself any longer.

The other men moved back into the audience, and McKenna got to her feet, stalking closer to Tag, who was beckoning her with the crook of his finger.

She moved up against him, their noses nearly touching as he continued to grind his body against hers. She could hardly breathe for wanting him, a desperate ache infusing her blood. He was the hottest man she'd ever laid eyes on, and tonight, he'd gone above and beyond. She'd known from the get-go that Tag wouldn't be comfortable with this, but here he was, working it like a pro.

His arms went around her, his hands cupping her ass and jerking her forward as he leaned in, his lips brushing her ear.

"Do you know how bad I want to fuck you right now?" he asked.

McKenna nodded. She did know because she felt the same.

"I want you to ride my cock."

Knowing they were in public and she couldn't very well do that, McKenna allowed herself the fantasy for a moment while he squatted in front of her, his mouth and hands traveling up her body slowly as he returned to his full height.

"Holy shit," she breathed out when he was looking down at her.

The song faded, more cheers erupted, and McKenna stood staring at her future husband. She was grinning from ear to ear, as was Tag.

"So? What'd you think?" Sam called from behind her.

"I think…" McKenna kept her eyes locked with Tag's. "That you're gonna do that for me again real soon."

"Only next time," Tag added as he leaned in close, "we'll be alone, and you *will* ride my cock."

A flash of heat consumed her as he looked at her mouth before he pulled her in and crushed his lips to hers.

McKenna gave in, as she always did. Only this time, she started counting down the minutes until they could do this again.

Because … damn … that had been the hottest thing she'd seen in her entire life.

"Okay, you two lovebirds," Sierra said from close by. "Looks like your rendezvous will have to be postponed."

McKenna pulled her mouth from Tag's and glanced over at her friend, lifting her eyebrows in question.

"Tomorrow's your wedding day. And you know the rule. The groom can't see the bride. So that means we'll be stayin' with you tonight. And he"—Sierra glanced over at Tag—"will be stayin' with the boys."

The disappointment of not being with Tag tonight was overwhelmed by the anticipation that flooded her.

They were getting married tomorrow.

Holy shit.

They were *finally* getting married.

Chapter *Eight*

Saturday afternoon
The wedding

Sierra stood beside Logan, waiting for Tag to make his way up to the altar after walking McKenna's mother to her seat. The scene before her made her smile. So many people, all gathered together in one place, all patiently waiting for the ceremony to begin.

Surprisingly, Sierra wasn't nervous, merely eager for them to get on with it. She had spent the morning with McKenna, along with Sam and Mercedes, helping her to get ready, trying to calm her nerves, and ultimately making her laugh. They'd arranged for breakfast to be delivered to the cabin, not wanting to risk Tag seeing McKenna before he was supposed to. It had been a fun, laughter-filled morning, but Sierra was as anxious as Tag and McKenna to get this started.

She was excited for this day, excited for two of her nearest and dearest friends to pledge their love for one another. Today, Sierra was McKenna's matron of honor, while Logan stood for Tag as his best man. The couple had opted to keep the wedding party small, due to the fact there were so many people close to McKenna, and the woman didn't seem to know how to pick one person for the high honor without selecting everyone.

So, to make it simple, last night after the striptease, they'd come up with a plan to make it easy. Everyone's name went into a hat—two separate ones, actually—and McKenna and Tag then drew randomly. Not conventional, maybe, but it had been fun. Probably more so because Sierra's name had been selected, and she had the honor of standing up for the couple as they stated their vows to one another.

Once Tag made his way to the altar, standing in front of the officiant who'd entered from the side of the beautifully decorated chapel, a silence descended over the group gathered before her. Luckily, they'd had an assigned wedding coordinator who'd handled all of the details, right down to the decorations, as well as the menu, cake, flowers, and music. Sierra merely oversaw it all, ensuring that nothing was missed.

Pretty much, the only thing the rest of them had to do was show up.

Which they'd all done, including Tag's father and his stepmother.

"Ready?" Logan whispered as he leaned down toward her.

"Absolutely." Sierra allowed Logan to lead them down the aisle. When they arrived at the altar, she went to the left, Logan to the right.

As Sierra took her place, she heard laughter and turned in time to see Hannah marching down the aisle, grinning from ear to ear as she tossed rose petals onto the floor behind her. She was so animated, making Sierra laugh along with the others. When she made her way to the front, Cole snatched her up and pulled her into his lap, making Hannah giggle in response.

Sierra's attention was drawn to the back of the room, and tears formed in her eyes as she saw McKenna and her father, Jason, come into view.

Since McKenna hadn't known what was happening, Sierra had called Diane, asking McKenna's mother to do the honors of selecting what she thought her daughter would like. The dress was perfect. McKenna looked stunning. Her ivory vintage gown, with top-applied flowers on illusion tulle, sheer three-quarter sleeves, and a full, layered skirt, looked as though it had been made with McKenna in mind. Elegant and beautiful, just like McKenna.

The music began, and Jason led McKenna down the aisle while there were gasps as everyone took her in. Sierra glanced over at Tag, noticing the man was motionless, his eyes glued to the woman as she approached him. The look on his face was priceless, and hopefully someone thought to get a candid shot of what true adoration looked like, because that was the only way to describe it.

McKenna and her father stopped at the altar.

"Who gives this woman to this man in marriage?" the officiant asked.

"Her mother and I do," Jason said gruffly, emotion clogging his voice.

McKenna stepped forward, as did Tag, both of them meeting in the middle. Jason then took McKenna's right hand from his left arm and placed it on Tag's left hand.

Sierra knew she wasn't going to make it through the ceremony without tears. She only hoped she didn't make a spectacle of herself when she did. Considering her hormones were on the fritz, hopefully she'd be forgiven if that did, in fact, happen.

While she tried to maintain her composure, Sierra reached for the bouquet when McKenna turned to hand it to her and then watched as Tag and McKenna both turned toward the officiant.

"Dear family and friends, we are gathered here today to witness and celebrate the union of Tag Murphy and McKenna Thorne in marriage. Through their time together, this couple has come to realize that their personal hopes and dreams are more attainable and more meaningful through mutual support, providing in love, commitment, and family. And so, they have decided to live their lives together as husband and wife.

"True marriage is more than the joining of two persons; it is the union of two hearts. It lives on the love you give each other and never grows old, but thrives on the joy of each new day. Marriage is love. May you always be able to talk things over, to confide in each other, to laugh with each other, to enjoy life together, and to share moments of quiet and peace, when the day is done. May you be blessed with a lifetime of happiness and a home of warmth and understanding."

Yep, Sierra knew the waterworks were about to start up, especially when she noticed McKenna's hand shaking as she held Tag's.

"Do you, Tag, take McKenna to be your lawfully wedded wife, promising to love and cherish, through joy and sorrow, sickness and health, and whatever challenges you may face, for as long as you both shall live?"

"I do," Tag said, his eyes lingering on McKenna's face.

"And do you, McKenna, take Tag to be your lawfully wedded husband, promising to love and cherish, through joy and sorrow, sickness and health, and whatever challenges you may face, for as long as you both shall live?"

"I do," McKenna replied, her voice shaky.

The officiant continued, "You have for each other special rings—symbols that love is the most precious element in your life together. The ring has no beginning and no end, which symbolizes that the love between you will never cease. You place these rings upon each other's fingers as a visible sign of your vows this day, which will make you husband and wife."

Sierra choked back a sob as McKenna and Tag turned to face one another. The two of them exchanged rings, reciting the words, "I give you this ring, a symbol of my love, as I give to you all that I am and accept from you all that you are."

"And now, by the power vested in me, I hereby pronounce you husband and wife. Tag, you may now kiss your bride."

Cheers erupted when Tag melded his lips to McKenna's, cupping her face in his big hands. Sierra then lost the battle to hold back the tears as she smiled at her friends, silently wishing them all the happiness the world could afford them.

"Family and friends, I present to you Mr. and Mrs. Tag Murphy."

Chapter *Nine*

McKenna felt weightless, as though nothing could touch her as she floated along. Everything since the moment she'd said I do had coalesced into a whirlwind of conversation and activity. And now, as they all sat at the formal reception dinner, enjoying fantastic wine and finishing a superb meal, the reality of the day was setting in.

She hadn't released Tag's hand since he'd walked her back down the aisle, and she wasn't sure she'd be able to release him for the rest of the night. It had made eating rather difficult, but her need to touch him had outweighed her need for food.

"Isn't the best man supposed to make a speech?" Luke called out, glancing down the table at Logan.

"He is," Logan confirmed with a smirk.

McKenna smiled as Logan got to his feet, adjusting his tuxedo jacket and turning his attention to the entire group.

"I'm going to preface this by saying that I did ask Tag if there was anything I shouldn't say. He said no. So, for the record, that's on him."

McKenna laughed, thinking of all the things that Logan could say, things that she should be worried about, but she came up with nothing. This was Logan; although he might tease, she knew he would be respectful.

"Okay, so first things first. I'd like to start out by mentioning that McKenna looks stunning today. Then again, that's not much different than any other day, although she does have an impressive glow about her today. As for the guy next to her… Well, my grandfather always said if you can't say anything nice, then shut the hell up. But he's not here today, so I'll keep going." Logan's grin widened as he looked at Tag. "However, in Tag's defense, where he lacks in looks, he certainly makes up for in personality… No, wait. Not personality. He makes up for it in smarts. Yes. The guy's damn smart. I'm sure no one can disagree with me. Especially today of all days when he made the smartest decision of his life and married McKenna."

The group laughed, as Logan had obviously intended. McKenna squeezed Tag's hand and looked over at him. God, she loved this man.

"By luck of the draw, I was given the coveted honor of being Tag's best man on this special day, and though my first reaction was to rub it in everyone's face, the truth is, it really is an honor for me. I've known Tag for some time now, and I've grown to respect him. Not only because he's been my legal representation on multiple occasions but also because I consider him a friend.

"I'm proud to stand here and celebrate one of Tag's greatest accomplishments to date. Marrying McKenna, devoting all of the love, respect, and friendship that he has within him to her, his wife and best friend. And as I'm sure everyone else here would agree, we're honored to be here, to celebrate this incredible day with you."

Logan reached for his wineglass, lifting it up as he peered over at them. "Here's to a lifetime of happiness, and the kind of deep love that comes from finding the one person who completes you, who makes you whole. Congrats."

McKenna couldn't stop the tears as glasses clinked in their honor. Today had been more than she'd ever anticipated.

After Logan's toast, they'd resumed their conversations as the waiters came to clear the table. Although the attention was supposed to be on them, Tag couldn't hold back the question he had for Luke. He was still wondering where the man's optimism came from, but after seeing Sierra earlier, he was pretty sure he'd finally figured it out.

"So, Luke," Tag began. "I'm still curious as to the change in you."

"What change?" Luke smirked, glancing over at Sierra and Cole.

"You told me last night that you only live once. While I agree, it's not a perspective I'd have pegged you for."

"I turned over a new leaf," he said.

"Yeah?" Tag asked, looking over at Sierra with a grin. "So there's news?"

Luke lifted his eyebrows, but the smile never left his face. "What news?"

"I know those two make you happy, but I think you're hidin' somethin'. Care to share?"

Luke looked at Sierra, and Tag caught her slight nod. When Luke met his gaze again, there was something else there. Pride.

"This is supposed to be your day, so we were waiting to tell everyone."

The table went silent around them.

"We're pregnant," Luke told them proudly.

Silence descended on the table briefly, but then there was a round of clapping and cheers as people were instantly out of their seats, hugging Sierra and clapping Luke and Cole on the back. Tag and McKenna joined in the celebration, going over to Luke directly.

Lifting his wineglass to Luke, Tag tilted it toward him. "Congrats. Just another reason for us to celebrate today."

Luke nodded, another smile tilting the corner of his mouth.

The instrumental music started, a subtle hint for the next phase of tonight's program, causing a hush to come over the group.

"I think that's our cue," Tag stated, turning his attention to his ... wife—God, he loved the sound of that. Face-to-face with McKenna, Tag smiled. "Dance with me," he suggested to McKenna, his fingers still linked with hers.

As was planned, "All of Me" by John Legend began when Tag led McKenna out onto the floor. He pulled her in close, his eyes locked with hers.

His wife.

When tears filled McKenna's eyes, he reached up and brushed one away.

"You are the absolute most beautiful woman on the face of the earth. I just thought you should know that."

McKenna sobbed softly, another tear escaping. "Thank you."

"I love you," he whispered.

"I love you, too," she said softly. "So much."

Pulling her close to him, Tag moved around the dance floor. This time, as all eyes were on him dancing, he didn't care. It didn't matter to him who saw. He wanted the world to watch, to know just how much he loved this woman, how overwhelmingly happy she made him. This was, by far, the greatest day of his entire life.

A few minutes later, the song faded away but quickly transitioned into another, and that was when McKenna's father came over, asking for permission to cut in. Tag placed McKenna's hand in her father's and turned to find McKenna's mother standing on the sideline. He moved toward her, reaching for her hand.

With a beaming smile, Diane accepted his offer.

"Today was perfect," Diane told him as they moved slowly around the dance floor, allowing McKenna and her father to maintain the spotlight.

"She's perfect," Tag told her.

Diane smiled up at him. "I'm so glad she found you."

Tag grinned. "Me, too."

He remembered back when he'd met McKenna. She'd been the persistent journalist who'd done her best to interfere in his life, trying to get the dirt on him and the McCoys. She was good at what she did, there was no doubt about it, and it hadn't taken long for Tag to find himself infatuated with her. That feeling had only intensified over time.

"You do know that I'm waiting for the two of you to give me grandbabies," Diane said with a chuckle.

Tag laughed, his gaze cutting to McKenna's. If everything went well, hopefully his mother-in-law wouldn't be waiting long.

When the song ended, Jason came over and asked if he could cut in, making Tag smile. "Should I be worried that you keep stealing women from me?"

Jason laughed as he pulled Diane against him. "Just wait until y'all give me granddaughters."

Tag could not wait for that day. When he turned to find McKenna, intending to go back to her, he found her dancing with his father, Jackson. For a brief moment, Tag was stunned, unable to move. While he tried to process what he was seeing, Victoria came up to him, an uncertain smile on her face.

His manners returned, and he instantly asked her to dance, moving closer to his stepmother. They danced in silence for a moment because Tag had no idea what to say.

Luckily, Victoria eased some of the tension when she said, "He loves you. I'll admit, he has a very strange way of showing that, but truth is, he does love you."

It was the first time that Victoria had ever said that to him. Most of their conversations were short and to the point. The rare times he found himself around his father, they generally talked about work.

"Thank you for coming," Tag said. "It means a lot that he's here."

"He wouldn't have missed it. He just doesn't know how to show that side of himself."

Tag nodded. His father had never been the type to dole out love, or to even make Tag feel welcome, but there was one positive in all that. Tag had learned, through his own experiences, what not to do. And sometimes, that was as good a lesson as any.

The song slowly began to fade. "It's time you go back to your bride," Victoria said as she released his hand.

Turning, he saw McKenna smiling up at Jackson, looking slightly uncomfortable, but the woman never ceased to amaze him. She handled any situation brilliantly, including this one.

Making his way over to her, he pulled her against him as the rest of the crowd moved onto the dance floor with them, joining in as another slow song started.

"Thank you," he told her.

"For?"

"For being my greatest accomplishment to date. For making me the happiest man in the world. For … being you."

Two hours later, Tag was trying to find a way to sneak out and take McKenna back to their cabin. He was seeking her out when his father approached, his expression sober.

"Dad," Tag said calmly when Jackson came to stand directly in front of him.

"I didn't want to take too much of your time," Jackson said, his gaze sliding across the room to where McKenna was talking to Sierra, Sam, and Mercedes. "I just wanted a chance to talk to you. In private."

Tag lifted his brow in question.

"I wanted to tell you…" Jackson thrust his hands into his pockets, his face contorting into what appeared to be pain.

"You don't have to say it," Tag told him, hating to see his father hurting.

"Yes. I do," Jackson said firmly, looking directly into Tag's eyes.

"I've never been the best father. I know that. I've never tried to make excuses for my shortcomings, but I do want you to know that I … I'm proud of you, Tag. I've always been proud of you. Despite the type of father I've been, you've… You're a good man. One I admire."

Tag didn't move. Hell, he wasn't sure he was even breathing. It was the first time in all his life that his father had come out and said anything regarding how he'd been as a father.

The silence lingered between them for a moment before Tag managed to croak out a thank you.

"You're welcome. And I really am proud of you. She's an incredible woman. And you're lucky to have each other."

"That we are," Tag agreed.

Jackson's hand slipped from his pocket. He then placed it on Tag's shoulder, and for a moment, he expected a pat but was shocked when Jackson pulled him close, both arms circling him as he hugged him.

"I love you, son."

Tag swallowed hard, his eyes closing as he hugged his father back. The emotion that churned in his chest surprised him. Perhaps he'd never expected his father to say any of these things, and he wasn't sure how to process them. But he knew one thing for sure, so he said, "I love you, too, Dad."

When Jackson pulled back, they stood staring at one another for a moment. It wasn't awkward, as Tag had expected it to be. Jackson then smiled, a genuine grin that transformed his usually stoic features. "Like I said, I'm so proud of you."

Tag nodded. "Thank you," he said, his voice guttural with the emotion now clogging his throat.

Jackson turned and surveyed the room. When he turned back, he once again looked like the father he'd known his whole life, somber, expressionless.

"I should let you get back to your wife," Jackson said.

Another nod was all Tag could offer. Although his father had shut down once again, the moment they'd shared had been real and something Tag had needed more than he had realized.

"Thanks, Dad."

It was Jackson's turn to nod before he silently walked away.

Tag remained rooted in that same spot for long minutes after Jackson disappeared into the group, taking it all in.

He glanced at McKenna. His ... *wife*. Holy hell—at the risk of repeating himself—he definitely loved the sound of that.

She was smiling at her friends, laughing and joking, but then her gaze slid to his briefly. Another smile—one filled with promise and meant only for him—tilted her lips.

Definitely time to get her back to the room. Tag was ready to call it a night, but not because he was tired.

Nope, sleeping was the last thing on his mind.

Chapter *Ten*

By the time Tag got McKenna back to their cabin, he was having a difficult time keeping his hands off her. And by difficult, he meant damn near impossible.

They'd stayed at the reception longer than he'd intended. Not that he hadn't had a good time celebrating with his friends and family, but from the instant McKenna had looked into his eyes and said that she would be his wife, he hadn't thought of anything other than celebrating with her.

Naked.

"Dress. Off. Now," he growled after flipping the lock on the door.

The seductive glimmer in McKenna's eyes made his dick harder than granite. He stalked her across the living area and right into the bedroom.

"Unzip me," she said sweetly, turning to face away from him.

Tag slipped the zipper down her back, places kissing along the skin he exposed. While she pulled her arms from the sleeves, he unhooked her bra, not wanting to waste another second before burying himself so deep inside her she felt him everywhere.

After shrugging out of his jacket, he proceeded to strip. Kicking off his shoes, working the buttons on his shirt, and then finally removing his slacks, underwear, and socks. When he was completely naked, Tag grabbed McKenna around the waist, spinning her and then tumbling them both to the bed, her on top. But that didn't last long because he was desperate for her. They had all night, but for now, he wanted to be inside her.

McKenna clutched his head, pulling his lips to hers as she moaned sweetly into his mouth, her tongue darting out to meet his. Tag focused on the kiss, savoring the sweet taste of her while he guided himself to her entrance.

With practiced ease, he slid inside her slowly. As slowly as he could manage anyway.

"Tag!" she said on a breathless moan, her lips still pressed to his.

"Feel me," he whispered, pulling back and staring down at her. "Feel me inside you, filling you, loving you."

McKenna's arms wreathed his neck, pulling him down to her until they were touching everywhere.

"So good," McKenna moaned. "Love feeling you inside me."

Tag pumped his hips forward, retreating slowly and lodging deep once again. Her body sheathed him in warmth, her inner walls clutching him tightly.

"One of these days…" Tag said, pumping his hips, "we're going to have babies."

McKenna's smile was luminous, making her entire face glow as she locked her gaze with his.

"Lots of babies," she replied. "And the more we practice, the better our chances."

God, he loved this woman. She was his best friend, his soul mate, the love of his life, and now his wife. And yes, one of these days, hopefully sooner rather than later, she'd be the mother of his children.

"Love me, Tag," she pleaded, her legs wrapping around him as she dug her ankles into his lower back.

Tag thrust into her, keeping a languorous pace, enjoying the feel of her body clutching him tightly. He pressed his mouth to hers once more, using his tongue to mimic the motion of his hips. McKenna's arms dropped down to his sides and then beneath his own. The next thing he knew, she was digging her nails into his ass, pulling him forward as she cradled his hips between her knees. He didn't increase the pace at first, instead screwing his hips, burying his cock deeper into her wet heat, loving the way she moaned his name, begging for more.

He lifted his head, their eyes locking as he began fucking her harder, faster, impossibly deeper.

"McKenna. Baby," he whispered, breathless. "I love you. God, I love you."

"I love you, too," she said, her nails digging deeper into his skin as she pulled him closer.

He retreated again, then plunged into her, rocking his hips forward and back, never wanting this moment to end but knowing he was going to come any second, especially if she kept doing that… The way her inner muscles tightened, gripping him, milking him… There was no way he could hold back.

Slamming his mouth to hers once more, he pounded into her, his arms tensing as he held himself above her.

Tag swallowed McKenna's cries of pleasure as she came apart. Her orgasm triggered his, and he stilled, lodged as deep inside her as he could possibly be.

After they showered together, McKenna curled up in Tag's strong arms, her head resting on his chest, the gentle thump of his heartbeat beneath her ear. The room was dark, and she could feel the gentle rock of the boat while she replayed the events of the last few days, mostly the events of the night.

"I saw you talking to your father," McKenna prompted, remembering the serious conversation she'd witnessed from across the room.

"He wanted to congratulate us," Tag said simply, but McKenna could tell he was holding something back.

"So it was a good discussion?" she inquired.

"It was," he assured her. "He told me he loved me."

McKenna's heart constricted. She knew how strained their relationship was, and she was grateful that Jackson had the good sense to reach out to Tag. It was long overdue, that was for sure.

Her mind drifted back to the evening. The time she'd spent with family and friends, laughing, joking, celebrating… It seemed surreal, as though she'd spent endless days in a fairy tale. One she never wanted to come to an end. She still had a hard time wrapping her mind around the fact that she and Tag were married, but…

They. Were. Married.

She was now Mrs. Tag Murphy.

It had been a dream of hers for so long, she was almost tempted to pinch herself to see if she was actually awake. Her thumb drifted over the new diamond-encrusted band adorning the finger on her left hand, and she smiled, thinking about the matching platinum band on Tag's finger. She'd been pleasantly surprised with his selection, but then again, the man did have exquisite taste.

"What are you thinking about?" Tag asked. "I can tell you're smilin'."

"You. Me. Us." She couldn't stop thinking about it.

She wondered whether every bride felt like this on their wedding day. Completely content, heart full to bursting … loved, cherished. Adored.

Yes, that was what she was feeling. *Adored.*

"I adore you," McKenna said softly. "I think it's more than love."

Tag kissed the top of her head, his fingers sliding through her hair. "Adored. I like that."

Another smile tipped her lips as she listened to Tag's strong heartbeat, his steady inhale and exhale.

Tomorrow they'd be going back to the real world, getting back to life in the fast lane. But for some reason, McKenna had a feeling things would be different for them. This was the first day of the rest of their lives.

However, before they got to that point, McKenna wasn't ready for the night to end.

Lifting her head, she grinned into the darkness. She could barely make out Tag's profile, but she could tell he was looking at her. Instead of saying a word, she simply crawled beneath the blankets and decided to give him something else to remember about this day.

Chapter *Eleven*

Two months later

"McKenna? I'm home." Tag placed his laptop on the kitchen table, removing his suit jacket and loosening his tie. "Where are you?" he called out when she didn't answer.

"In here!"

Tag grinned. He didn't know exactly where *here* was, but he followed the sound of her voice to the master bedroom. However, she wasn't there, so he peeked into the bathroom to see her standing in front of the sink, staring down at the counter.

"What're you doin'?" he asked, moving toward her.

McKenna's eyes lifted to his and he noticed tears in them.

"What's wrong?" he instantly asked, concern filling his chest.

She turned to face him fully, her hands trembling but a smile tipping the corners of her mouth. "We're pregnant."

His gaze fell to the counter, where he noticed a white stick lying on a paper towel. He allowed the words to sink in, tossing them around in his head for a moment as warmth filled his entire being.

"We're...?"

McKenna cleared the few steps between them, throwing her arms around his neck and latching on tightly. "We're pregnant. We're pregnant," she exclaimed, peppering his face with kisses.

A tortured laugh ripped from his chest as he realized what she was telling him. Tag wrapped his arms around her, lifted her off her feet, and kissed her lips. "We're gonna have a baby?"

"Yes," she said, her smile radiant, her tears glistening down her cheeks. "We're gonna have a baby."

"Have you told your parents?" he asked, setting her down on her feet, a nervous energy filling him as he thought about all the things they needed to do in order to prepare for a baby. They needed a nursery, a crib, baby clothes...

"Relax," McKenna said with a chuckle, gripping his wrists. "At the most, we're six weeks along. The first thing we have to do is go to the doctor to confirm."

Tag nodded, an endless list starting in his head. Bottles, diapers, car seats...

"We've got plenty of time," she told him, her hand coming up to smooth his forehead. "No need to start freaking out just yet."

Tag laughed.

Him? Freaking out? No way was he...

Okay, so yes, he was freaking out, but this was the best news he'd heard all week.

They were pregnant.

His gaze lowered to her flat belly and his hands followed suit. He lifted her shirt and flattened his palm over her warm skin. A baby.

They stood in silence for a few minutes, McKenna's hands coming to rest over his as they stared back at one another.

"So, first we go to the doctor? Then what?"

"Well, technically, *first*, we should go in there," McKenna replied, nodding toward the bedroom. "And then, after you make love to me, we'll have dinner, go to bed, spend the weekend doing whatever we want, and first thing Monday morning, when the doctor's office opens, I'll call and make an appointment. *Then* we'll go see the doctor."

Tag smirked. The woman knew him so well, she had to have known this would be how he'd react, yet she appeared calm and collected and, yes, glowing with excitement.

Reaching around behind her, he cupped her ass, pulled her to him, and then lifted her off her feet. Her arms came up to ring his neck as her legs wrapped around his waist. "I heard the make love to me part," he told her. "Once we're done with that, then you can repeat everything that's supposed to happen afterward."

McKenna laughed, her lips coming down to rest on his gently. "I can do that. I can definitely do that."

Tag carried her into the bedroom, gently laying her down on the bed.

"I'm not gonna break," she told him, grabbing his wrists and jerking him forward. "And no way you're gonna get away with treating me like fine china for the next seven and a half months."

Tag's eyes instantly drifted to her belly as he tried to remain upright.

"Tag Murphy…" McKenna hissed, causing him to look up into her eyes. "Get on this bed right this instant and fuck me senseless. Then you can make me dinner."

Without hesitating, Tag reached for her cotton shorts, the ones she wore around the house when she wanted to get comfortable, and ripped them down her legs, taking her panties with them. She did the same with her shirt, pulling it over her head and throwing it at him.

It only took a minute for him to undress, and once he was naked, he ordered her to get on her knees.

"Yes, sir," she said, her tone raspy.

McKenna turned over and got to her hands and knees, pushing her sweet ass in his direction. Tag placed his hands on her ass, pushing her forward just enough that he could bury his tongue in her pussy, making her cry out as she bucked against him, her sounds muffled when she buried her face in the blankets.

He ate her until she screamed his name, coming hard and fast. Before she settled down, he was kneeling on the bed behind her, guiding his cock to her pussy. He didn't slam into her, because no matter what she said, he wasn't going to be quite that rough, but he wasn't gentle, either. Once she was stretched around him, he began fucking her. He wasn't going slow, not attempting to draw this out, because he was quickly getting lost in the pleasure of her body.

His balls drew up tight, his cock pulsing as he continued to tunnel into her wet heat, fucking her as though he'd never get the chance again. He could see their reflection in the mirror above the dresser, watching as he pounded into her, her beautiful breasts swaying with every thrust.

When she lifted her head, meeting his gaze in the mirror, he locked his eyes with hers and smiled. The naughty look she sent his way only brought him closer to the edge, but he didn't waver, continuing to fuck her. He wouldn't come until she did, and he wasn't going to rush her. It felt too good; being inside her felt like heaven and he never wanted it to end.

"Tag," McKenna said, the single word coming out on a breathless moan. "You're"—*thrust*—"gonna"—*thrust*—"make"—*thrust*—"me come! Fuck yes!"

"That's it," he growled as he let himself go, filling her as she milked his dick with her sweet body.

When he dropped to the bed beside her, she eased over him. "That was fantastic," she told him, still sounding as though she'd run a marathon.

"You're welcome," he told her with a grin.

McKenna chuckled. "God, I love you. No wait, I take that back."

Tag knew what she was going to say, but he waited to hear it anyway.

"I *adore* you," she said, pressing her lips gently to his.

"I adore you right back," he whispered, wrapping her in his arms, ready to give in to sleep.

"Nuh-uh," she said, tapping his chest with her palm. "It's your night to cook dinner. And I'm starving."

Tag groaned, his eyes closed.

"And no frozen pizza tonight."

"No?" he asked, thinking that sounded about perfect since it was easy.

"Nope. I'm thinking... I don't know. Maybe steak and baked potato."

Tag opened his eyes, peering up at her. "Really?"

McKenna nodded. "Yes. Since you're cooking and because I'm eating for two. Wouldn't be fair to make us live on frozen pizza, now would it?"

Tag smirked at his wife. His beautiful, sweet, manipulative wife. "No, it wouldn't be fair. Not fair at all."

With that, he spanked her on the ass and catapulted himself out of bed, heading straight for the kitchen.

"You're naked!" she called out from the bedroom.

He stuck his head back in the room. "And I'm gonna remain that way, because one day, we'll have little ones running around and I won't be able to do it anymore."

"Good point," she said, closing her eyes as she smiled. "Very good point."

Yep, he thought so, too.

Epilogue

Ten years later

McKenna relaxed on the lounge chair, letting the sun beat down on her face as she tried to get comfortable, grateful for a few minutes of peace and quiet.

"How did I know you'd be here?"

Opening her eyes, she peered up at Tag through the darkened lenses of her sunglasses, smiling as she did. "Lucky guess?"

Tag chuckled, dropping onto the chair beside her, kicking his feet up onto the chair and sighing heavily.

"Remember the last time we were on a cruise?" she asked him a few minutes later.

"I'll never forget it," he replied, sounding as tired as she felt.

"We spent our time in the casino and the hot tub…" she muttered.

"Those were the days."

"They certainly were."

Allowing her mind to drift back to that day, she remembered all the wicked things Tag had done to her before and after they were married. She felt herself drifting off to sleep, the dream world blocking out the real world for a few minutes as she imagined herself sleeping in late, waking to find Tag watching her. Dream McKenna rolled over, placing kisses on Dream Tag's chest, easing herself beneath the blankets so that she could…

A high-pitched shriek had McKenna sitting up, looking around to see where the sound came from. And that was when she saw him…

Mickey Mouse.

Of course.

This wasn't *that* cruise.

This was an entirely different one.

"Mommy! Look who it is!" Janey squealed as she came running over to McKenna. Bracing herself for her three-year-old, McKenna caught her when she propelled herself into her lap, pointing at the big guy with mouse ears, a huge grin, and a pair of swim trunks making his way through the crowd of children anxious to meet their favorite cartoon character.

Funny how Mickey Mouse was still an icon at this point in time. McKenna figured he always would be.

The closer the mouse came, the tighter Janey's hands clasped McKenna. Her daughter was fond of the character, but clearly she preferred to keep him at a safe distance. McKenna wrapped her arms around her little girl, holding her tightly, letting her know she wasn't going to let go.

"Where's your brother?" she asked, looking around to see where her nine-year-old had slipped off to.

"He's trying to talk to Mickey," Janey informed her, bouncing on her lap.

"I see him," Tag informed her, sitting up in his chair. "So much for that nap, huh?" He grinned over at her.

"We have that mouse to thank for that," she informed him, laughing as she planted kisses on Janey's head, brushing her vibrant red hair out of her face.

"Levi!" Tag called to their son. When the handsome, dark-haired kid glanced their way, his face lit up before his attention returned to the giant mouse making the kids laugh.

Although Tag was right, that nap they'd been trying to take wasn't going to happen at this point, McKenna couldn't find it in her to be disappointed. This was life as she knew it.

Two incredible kids who provided the sunshine in her world, an amazing husband she adored, a week at sea, and a big giant mouse...

What more could she ask for?

♥□□□♥□□□♥

I hope you enjoyed the follow up to Tag and McKenna's story. Adored is #10 in the Club Destiny series. Want to see some fun stuff related to the Club Destiny series, you can find extras on my website. Or how about what's coming next? I keep my website updated with the books I'm working on, including the writing progression of what's coming up for Club Destiny.

www.NicoleEdwardsAuthor.com

If you're interested in keeping up to date on Club Destiny as well as receiving updates on all that I'm working on, you can sign up for my monthly newsletter.

Want a simple, *fast* way to get updates on new releases? You can sign up to receive text message notifications on my website as well. I promise not to spam your phone. This is just my way of letting you know what's happening because I know you're busy, but if you're anything like me, you always have your phone on you.

And last but certainly not least, if you want to see what's going on with me each week, sign up for my weekly Hot Sheet! It's a short, entertaining weekly update of things going on in my life and that of the team that supports me. We're a little crazy at times and this is a firsthand account of our antics.

Did you know that my Club Destiny and Alluring Indulgence series overlap? You can find the reading order on my website as well.

Keep reading for an excerpt from Wait for Morning, the
first in Nicole's Sniper 1 Security series.

Wait *for* Morning

A Sniper 1 Security Novel

Book One

Nicole Edwards

One

Thump-scrape-thump

Marissa Trexler came awake slowly, trying to fight the groggy feeling as she forced her eyes open. A quick glance at the blurry red digits on the alarm clock told her it was just after midnight. The dim light from the lamp on her bedside table, along with the Kindle resting on her chest, said she'd fallen asleep reading again.

She really needed to stop doing that. More than likely, the suspense novel she'd been engrossed in before she finally dozed off was making her paranoid. Stephen King had a way of doing that to a person.

Sliding the e-reader to the pillow beside her, Marissa scrubbed her eyes with the heels of her hands and glanced over at the bedroom door. Shut and locked. Exactly the way she'd left it. No boogeyman looming over her, ready to do whatever it was that boogeymen did.

She lay there, momentarily listening for the sound that had awoken her. Nothing.

Yep, just as she'd thought. Paranoid. *Thanks a lot, Mr. King.* Maybe it really was time to switch to some lighter reading at night. Perhaps her best friend, Courtney, was right, Marissa should try romance on for size.

Just when she reached for the lamp to shroud the room in darkness so she could attempt to get back to the blessed dreamless state she'd been in, Marissa stopped, her hand hovering inches from the lamp base.

Thump-scrape

Okay, maybe paranoid wasn't the right word because she clearly hadn't imagined the sound *that* time.

Glancing toward her bedroom door once more, Marissa tried to make sense of the noise, but she couldn't. It sounded almost as though someone was dragging something across the floor and then carelessly dropping it. Over and over again.

There was no way that could possibly be it, though.

Right?

Maybe it was the screen door. Yes, that made perfect sense. A much more likely culprit. The damn thing was always coming unlatched, a reoccurring problem with the blistering cold winds slamming brutally against her small rental—aka *safe* house—especially in the dead of winter.

Not for the first time, Marissa wished she was back in Texas. Back where the temperatures weren't freeze-your-nipples-off cold.

Figuring the screen door wouldn't fix itself, Marissa forced her legs over the edge of the bed and slid her feet into her cable-knit boot slippers.

Thump-scrape-thump

A frisson of fear sliced through her at the sound, making her toes curl against the faux fur encasing her feet and causing her heart to slam into her ribs. The screen door was never that consistent.

Swallowing past the lump of ice-cold terror lodged in her suddenly dry throat, Marissa managed to get to her feet. After grabbing her heavy robe from the chair beside the bed, she slowly slipped out of her bedroom, moving down the short, narrow hallway toward the front door as she pulled her robe over trembling arms. Forgoing the lights on her way, she kept her ears tuned to the sound.

Thump-scrape-thump

This time Marissa stopped midstride, standing a mere foot from the doorway that led to the living room as she tried to pinpoint the direction of the noise. It didn't sound like it was coming from the front of the house, which meant … the screen door wasn't the guilty party.

Thump-tha-thump

Thump-tha-thump

Swallowing hard, Marissa realized that new thumping sound was her heart—threatening to beat right out of her chest.

That realization didn't do a damn thing to help the oncoming panic attack.

Thump-scrape-thump

Shit.

Not her heart.

Oh, God!

Marissa listened for a moment, noticing the house was now void of all noise except for the soft rumble of heat through the air vents and the drumbeat coming from her chest. Was the sound coming from behind her? She tried to force her feet to move, but the overwhelming fear kept her rooted in place.

Before the direction to run could make it from her brain to her feet, a hard, firm hand came over her mouth, yanking her back against an equally hard, firm body.

The cobwebs of sleep still saturated her gray matter, making it difficult to register the need to scream, but instinct had her instantly trying to wiggle away.

No! Not again!

A muffled sound escaped her—anything more was hindered by the large palm crushed over her mouth—but it wasn't nearly loud enough to attract help. Or maybe that was the terror lodged in her throat keeping the sound at bay. Either way, she found herself desperately trying to suck in air, stumbling as the massive body behind her pulled her away from the living room, forcing her to shift her feet or fall to the floor.

And yes, she suddenly wondered whether the latter wasn't a bad idea. Getting away should've been her top priority, and Marissa was pretty sure it would've been if she could think clearly.

"Not a word," the deep voice whispered, warm breath brushing against her neck.

Well, that confirmed the answer to the first question that had popped into her head: *man or woman?* Definitely a man.

Low, gruff, familiar, the voice was an oddly soothing rumble against her ear. She recognized the timbre, the cadence, even the inflection, but thanks to the all-consuming dread roiling in the pit of her stomach, she couldn't place it. When she tried to turn, to see who he was, he simply held her flush to his body, continuing to ease them closer to the back door via the darkened kitchen.

"Stay calm. We've gotta get outta here."

His voice was calm, not at all threatening, and the strong arms surrounding her weren't gripping her painfully, but Marissa still questioned: *friend or foe?* She didn't know the right answer, probably because she was still paralyzed with fear.

While her common sense tried to come fully online, the intruder continued to lead her away from the front of the house, and for whatever reason, Marissa found herself complying. Something told her she needed to trust this man.

Less than a minute later, they were stepping outside, the icy winds battering her body, the snow instantly seeping through her slippers, freezing her feet. The blistering cold kick-started her brain, and she glanced at the ski-mask-clad man, who was now reaching for her hand as he rapidly backed away from the house, his intense gaze penetrating her, even though she couldn't even make out the color of his eyes in the inky darkness, darkened even more by the rapidly moving clouds temporarily blocking out the moon.

"Let's go, Marissa!" the man yelled, grabbing her hand and hauling her through the snow that densely covered her backyard.

Was it a good sign that he knew her name?

Okay, so maybe she should've been more worried about the fact that snow was now filling her slippers and saturating her pajama bottoms, or perhaps that she was willingly running *away* from the safety of her house with a man she only thought she should trust.

Unable to form words to argue or even to ask questions, Marissa ran. More accurately, she stumbled through the snow, dredging her way around to the side of the house as fast as she could behind the stranger dressed in black, his clothing of choice a stark contrast against the brilliant white landscape now lit by the moon. Her brain fumbled to make sense of what was going on as her slippered feet trudged through two feet of soft snow blanketing the ground. The gloved hand holding hers felt safe, but for a fraction of a second, she pondered whether she was actually running *toward* disaster rather than running *from* it.

A metallic *ping* sounded from close by, causing her to flinch at the same time her masked companion grabbed her, hauling her close to his solid body and using himself as a human shield, steering her in the direction he apparently wanted her to go.

"In!" the man commanded as they approached a dark SUV haphazardly parked along the side of her house.

Ping.

Ping. Ping.

Holy shit. Was someone *shooting* at them?

With her stupidity level possibly at an all-time high, Marissa didn't question him as he yanked open the driver's door and shoved her into the vehicle, she didn't try to pull away, and she didn't glance back at her house, either, when he yelled, "Other side!" and pushed her across the center console.

"Seat belt!" The brusque word echoed through the chilly interior of the SUV as the engine roared to life when her masked companion hopped in the driver's seat. With frozen fingers, Marissa fumbled with her seat belt while she prayed the heater would push something more than arctic air at her.

How long did it take for frostbite to set in?

Wow. And wasn't *that* an odd question to worry about at a time like this?

Hoping she wasn't going to find out, she forced the notion from her head.

Less than a minute later, Marissa wasn't worried about her numb fingers and toes or even what the sound had been that had woken her in the middle of the night. Her new interest was who this man was and where they were going.

When she turned to face him, ready to pelt him with those exact questions, Marissa was tossed around the front seat like a rag doll—despite the seat belt that was supposed to hold her in place—as he took a turn on what had to be two wheels. Fear gripped her once again as she grabbed for the *oh-shit* handle and held on for dear life. He obviously knew what he was doing, navigating the top-heavy vehicle in polar-like conditions, never taking his eyes off the road.

Chancing another glimpse in his direction, Marissa studied his profile despite the mask still covering his features, trying her best to look at him. *Really* look at him.

When he glanced over at her, tugging the mask off his head, allowing her to see his face for the first time since he'd arrived to whisk her out of the house, her breath lodged in her throat.

What the fuck?

"You're lucky I don't punch you right now," she told him grumpily, earning a chuckle from him.

Continuing to watch him, Marissa willed her heart to stop pounding, her breath to return to normal.

"Since when did they start sending in the big guns?" she muttered when she could breathe again, sarcasm and incredulity replacing the fear that had racked her for the past... According to the blue digits on the dashboard, only fifteen minutes had passed since she'd awoken to the noise.

He didn't respond.

Before Marissa could blast him for what had happened, there was an explosion that rocked the SUV. Twisting in her seat and peering through the tinted back window, she saw a fireball billowing in the chilly night air.

"Ohmygod... Ohmygod... Oh. My. God." Marissa turned to eyeball the man who'd come to her rescue. The *last* man she'd expected to see. The *very* man who had just saved her life. "Was that...?"

"Your house? Yeah," he offered with a slight edge. Although his rich, dark tone reflected a hint of sympathy, his white-gray eyes were hard as steel.

Her house, or rather the residence she'd inhabited for the last two and a half months, was now... *Shit.* It was now a fireball in the sky.

Spinning back around and shifting nervously in her seat, Marissa sucked air into her lungs, praying she wouldn't hyperventilate and pass out. Or maybe that would be better than dealing with this now. Who knew?

A firm hand landed on her back, thrusting her forward.

"Head between your knees, damn it. Don't you dare pass out on me, girl."

Girl? Was he serious right now?

Marissa had no choice but to obey his booming command, as he was simultaneously forcing her head toward the floorboard. Closing her eyes, she slowed her breaths, ignoring the way her hands trembled uncontrollably and her heart raced like a Kentucky Derby racehorse. A few minutes later, when she finally got her bearings, she sat up slowly and asked the one question she felt she'd been asking for far too long. "Who's after me now?"

Once again, no response. *Typical.*

She might never receive an honest answer to that, but at least Marissa had the answer to her earlier question…

Disaster.

Plain and simple.

That was exactly what she'd been running *toward.*

And disaster's name was Trace Kogan.

●《》●《》●《》●

Several houses down, parked on the dark street

Son. Of. A. Bitch.

Gripping the steering wheel with one hand, Barry Thompson pressed the phone to his ear, staring through the windshield at the unbelievable sight before him.

"If you're callin' to tell me you don't have the girl, we're going to renegotiate the terms of your employment," the grating voice on the other end of the line growled furiously, his usual succinct annunciations slipping, hinting at his Texas drawl.

The only terms of employment Barry knew of were either do the job and live or fail, which would naturally lead to the opposite. He didn't have to be an Ivy League graduate to figure that one out. And that meant what Barry had to tell the crotchety bastard was going to likely put him in a world of hurt.

"House is up in flames and she's gone, boss," Barry said, quickly relaying the details in as few words as possible.

"Where is she?"

"Kogan got to her first." Silence lingered on the line, but he didn't dare say another word. He knew better.

" *Which* Kogan?"

"Trace," he told the infuriated man.

And wasn't that just the shit. Trace *fucking* Kogan— the absolute last man he'd expected to see—had come to the rescue, saving the girl from what should've been a quick snatch and grab. As for the explosion… That had been Dennis's idea. A way to cover their tracks.

Barry swallowed hard, waiting for the tirade that was more than likely about to come. The guy who'd hired him to grab Marissa Trexler had a temper to rival all.

"Where's Dennis?"

"Dead," he answered simply. Barry wasn't absolutely certain of that fact, but based on Trace's deadly reputation and the flames licking high into the night sky, it was a relatively safe assumption that Dennis, his dumb ass of a partner—his most recent one, mind you—wasn't in the land of the living any longer.

A heavy sigh sounded on the other end of the line, followed by, "I. Want. Her. Found. And I fucking want her found now. You've had more than enough time."

A click sounded in his ear, signaling the end of the call. Setting the phone down in the cup holder, Barry stared at the orange blaze. The irritable asshole who'd hired him for this job was a first-class prick, but he was right about one thing: this had gone on long enough. Barry had been hired once again—after that failed attempt a year ago that had forced him to lie low for a while—to snatch Marissa and, like then, it seemed luck wasn't on his side.

Getting the girl was the end goal, at least according to the prick who'd hired him, but it looked as though Barry had another target to get rid of before he could accomplish that.

Turning up the heat, he gripped the cold steering wheel as he shoved the gearshift into drive, flipped on his headlights, and started down the road. If he was right, he knew Kogan wouldn't go far tonight, and Barry fully intended to beat the man to the punch.

As he drove, ignoring the house engulfed in flames in his peripheral vision, he let a plan form in his head.

Keep reading for an excerpt from Office Intrigue. The first from
Nicole's Office Intrigue series.

OFFICE *INTRIGUE*

One

BEEP-BA-BEEP.

"Son of a bitch."

It should be a crime to have to get up before six o'clock in the morning.

"Eight more minutes is all you get," I mumbled into my pillow, talking to myself as I smacked the snooze button on my phone.

Beep-ba-beep.

Eight minutes was not nearly long enough. It felt more like two.

And, okay, fine, it was safe to say I wasn't a morning person, but this was one of those rare days when it was necessary that I got up at the ass-crack of dawn. The worst time of the day as far as I was concerned. But it was a necessary evil, because unlike...*nobody*...I didn't crawl out of bed looking like a supermodel. That shit didn't really happen. To anyone.

I rolled onto my stomach and kicked the comforter off my bed and onto the floor. Getting rid of my warm cocoon was the only way to ensure I wouldn't snuggle down again and ignore the annoying *beep-ba-beep* that was supposed to be a signal to get my happy ass out of bed.

Of course, I still closed my eyes. That's what snooze buttons were for, right?

•

Beep-ba-beep.

"Craaaaaap!" I was jarred awake by that annoying sound once again, but this time procrastination was not my friend.

Before I could screw myself out of any more prep time, my feet hit the floor and my tired ass was vertical. I made a big production out of yawning and stretching as I marched groggily to the bathroom. Through the haze of sleep, I flipped on the shower before stripping off my pajama pants and tank top, leaving them on the floor to pick up later. It wasn't that I was a complete slob...okay, that was a lie, I was a complete slob. Especially when it came to laundry. Good thing I rarely had people over to my apartment.

During my shower, I had a moment of clarity as my hands drifted downward, soaping every inch of skin. It was time for me to schedule another waxing appointment. This realization did not make me happy. How could it? What sane woman enjoyed having her pubic hair brutally ripped from her nether region? Maybe there were people who were into that sort of torture, but I wasn't one of them.

However, it was a necessity. A woman had to be prepared for the day she ran into the man who would rock her world and tip her otherwise unsteady existence right on its axis.

Not that I was looking, of course. I had far better things to do than wait for Mr. Right Now to pop into my life and make anything tip or spin.

Okay, another lie.

I was on a roll today.

It was too early and I hadn't had coffee. That was my excuse.

When I was done in the shower, I cut the water off. One towel was used to dry my face, then went on my hair; the other was for drying me from neck to toe.

There.

The biggest portion of my morning routine was taken care of and that only cost me…

Thirty-four minutes.

"Shit, shit, shit."

I stared at myself in the mirror. Even I knew I should've had a little more energy. After all, I had a job interview in less than two hours, which meant I should've been darting around like it was the first day of school.

Unfortunately, mornings did not contain the fuel necessary to light a fire under my ass.

That meant I had to rush through my makeup, but first brushing my teeth was critical. If my dentist wasn't always on my ass about it, I would've skipped flossing, but I had to listen to my mother bitch about enough already. I didn't need to get a lecture about good dental hygiene, too.

"See, Mom?" I offered a toothy grin to my reflection. "All shiny and clean."

Once that was done, it was time to put my face on. I had to look good. It was a requirement. Admittedly, my resume wasn't exactly noteworthy, so it was imperative that I looked the part of a professional woman. How did the saying go? Fake it until you make it?

The makeup only took a few minutes, then on to drying my hair, which took a good twenty more thanks to the fact that I had so much of it. Then the flat iron to make the long strands shiny and straight. Finally, on to my clothes. A cute yet conservative black skirt and a white silk camisole paired with a charming yet uber-conservative blazer was the winner. Then I grabbed the best black heels I owned—a sexy little pair of Kate Spades that I couldn't live without when I saw them—and slipped them on my feet.

I was finally ready.

For coffee.

Clearly, I spent too much time on my morning ritual, but hey, I was twenty-four years old and jobless. The interview I had that day was going to be the last of many, I hoped. I'd only been on eight in the past two weeks, none of which had panned out, but I had high expectations for this one. It was one of the most prestigious PR firms in the city and they were looking for a secretary. Which I thought was the same thing as a receptionist, right? Different term, same job? At least I hoped so because I exceled at that, truly. I mean, I was born to talk on the phone, so yeah, I figured if nothing else, I had a damn good shot.

And maybe you were wondering why I didn't tell you what city I was in. Truth was, it didn't matter. If I did tell you, you might know it and that would take some of the intrigue out of my story. So, we'll keep that a secret as well as the name of the PR firm. After all, you might know that one too.

Back to getting ready.

I tossed my lip gloss into my clutch and grabbed my car key and cell phone before stopping in the kitchen.

The apartment I lived in wasn't very big. Nothing more than six hundred square feet, but it was in a good area of town, clean, and relatively inexpensive. And by relatively, I meant that I could afford it back when I had a job three weeks ago. If this didn't pan out, it was no longer going to be inexpensive. It was going to be available for the next tenant.

But I couldn't worry about that now because I had somewhere to be and not a lot of time to get there.

After pulling up my texting app on my phone, I shot a quick message to my friend Kristen.

Luci: *Heading to my interview. Wish me luck.*

When the coffeemaker brewed the single cup, I tossed in a little Equal and a few drops of creamer before popping a lid on the travel mug and heading for the door. As soon as I grabbed the knob, my phone buzzed.

Kristen: *You've got this one in the bag.*

I didn't know about all that, but I was grateful to my friend. She was the one who'd gotten me this interview and it couldn't have come at a better time.

If I was lucky, I'd make it on time and they would hire me.

If I wasn't lucky, I'd be moving in with my parents.

•

Traffic was a bitch, and I could only hope that this place validated parking because I couldn't imagine how much it was going to cost. Since I valeted, I figured it wouldn't be cheap, but hey. It was that or be late, and like I said, I needed this job if I planned to have a roof over my head and food in my belly. I wasn't a huge fan of ramen noodles, and let's face it, moving back in with my folks wasn't an option.

"May I help you, miss?"

My eyes cut over to see an older man squinting at me from his spot behind a long counter. He had one eyebrow, bushy and solid white, and it was currently hovering close to what used to be his hairline.

"I'm good, thank you!" My heels clicked loudly on the marble floors as I dashed toward the elevator.

I knew exactly what I was looking for and the sign by the elevator said I needed to head to the thirty-second floor. I punched the button for the elevator, then adjusted my blazer and tugged on my skirt. It was a little shorter than I remembered it being, but there was nothing I could do about it at that point. It was an interview, so I'd likely be sitting down for it. Plus, I was wearing underwear, so it wasn't like I was indecent.

The elevator finally arrived, and at that point, I was beginning to sweat. I had two minutes and if this wasn't the expressway up to the thirty-second floor, I probably wouldn't make it. The lift was empty, so I stepped inside and hit the thirty-two, making it light up, then turned and checked myself in the mirrors.

"Not bad," I said to my reflection as I smoothed my hand over my hair, then swiped around my lips with one finger while another fanned my lashes to de-clump the mascara and *poof.* I was ready.

Another deep breath and then the elevator dinged, signaling my arrival.

I squared my shoulders, planted a brilliant smile on my face, then stepped off into a plush lobby and noticed...

Nothing.

Seriously. Not a soul.

It was empty.

Like ghost-town empty.

The lights weren't even on, which was slightly disconcerting. I quickly located the switch on the wall and made my way over. A second later, the room lit up like the surface of the sun. Okay, maybe not that bright, but at least it was no longer giving me an eerie feeling.

I strolled over to the desk, where I assumed a receptionist (fancier name for a secretary, I was pretty sure) should sit. If all went well, that was going to be my desk. As for it being empty, it sort of made sense because the job position was currently open. But it would soon be filled. By me!

I was optimistic, I wouldn't lie.

Sure, I had some reasons to be. One, Kristen had recommended me for this position, and considering her clout, I felt confident her word went a long way. And two, my resume had plenty of receptionist experience. Provided they could overlook the fact that I'd held twelve jobs in the past three years, I should be a shoo-in. Although I hadn't been let go from any of my previous jobs, I knew it didn't bode well that I hopped from one place to the next. In my defense, I was still searching for something to make me happy, not quite finding it anywhere.

As for being qualified, I couldn't tell you because this particular job posting didn't have any requirements. It actually said: REQUIREMENTS TO BE PROVIDED AT TIME OF INTERVIEW.

Now, I knew that sounded a little odd, but like I said, my friend suggested I apply. Plus, this was a prestigious PR firm with a great reputation. I seriously doubted they were up to anything nefarious.

As I stood in the lobby, I wasn't sure what to do next.

Did I slip down the hall and peek into offices until I found someone?

Did I take a seat and wait for someone to come to me?

I'd never had this happen before.

So, I asked myself: If I worked at an esteemed PR firm and I was looking to hire a secretary, wouldn't I want someone who had ambition? A problem solver? Someone who could think on the fly?

Straightening my spine and adjusting my blazer, I decided that, yes, that was exactly what I would want. So, that was exactly what I'd be.

But before I did that, I figured I could check out the outer sanctum. The single glass desk held a phone and a calendar. Was it a blotter? I thought that's what they called it. Not that it mattered. I doubted there would be a vocabulary test. And if there was, it wasn't like I was a dummy.

To my right, there were three charcoal leather couches that were positioned in a U, facing the reception desk. A glass table that matched the desk sat in the center on a plush gray rug decorated with neon-colored geometric shapes. The walls were painted a light gray, decorated with metal geometric shapes that, yes, matched the patterns on the rug. Very artsy.

On the wall behind me, closest to the elevator, was a small counter—light gray cabinets, dark gray granite—with a fancy coffeemaker and little else. On my left was an opaque-glass wall that ran the length of the area and continued down what appeared to be a hallway. It was fairly bright behind the wall, likely from the windows, but there were no shadows, which made me believe there were no people working back there.

I guessed that was the way I should go.

Just when I started toward the hallway, the elevator dinged and I spun around, waiting to see who the newcomer might be.

When the doors opened, I found myself staring. Hard.

Four imposing figures stepped out, two at a time, all wearing suits. Not the cheap kind either. These were likely Armani or Gucci or possibly Tom Ford and definitely tailored.

The well-dressed men seemed to be deep in discussion, not one of them noticing me. It gave me a few seconds to take them all in, and let me just say, since this was going to be my job (there was that optimism again), I was going to be one happy girl getting to see these yummy treats every day.

There were two brunettes, a blond, and one who was shiny bald. Their skin tones ranged from pale to a sexy, rich chocolate color. If I had to venture a guess about their ages, I would've said from mid to late thirties. Their heights ranged from probably right at six feet to several inches taller. Then again, I was totally guessing about that. I wasn't a good judge of height. Being that I was five two without shoes, everyone was tall to me.

"Oh, uh," the blond said, coming to an abrupt halt when he peered up at me. His eyes darted to the reception desk, then back to me.

I couldn't tell if he was disappointed to find me standing there or if he'd expected someone else to be with me. Rather than allow the awkward silence to continue, I greeted the men, trying on my best receptionist voice. "I'm Luciana Wagner. I've got an interview this morning."

The blond looked at the brunettes, who—now that I got a good look at them—appeared to be identical twins. Probably close to six and a half feet tall, the two men had a rugged appeal that was heightened by the fact that they wore those expensive suits. Double yum.

Neither of them said anything. It was the dark-skinned, bald gentleman with the glowing brown eyes— *swoon!*—who stepped forward and held out his hand. He was long and lean, probably the smallest of the four men, but still impressively built. The slow smile that tilted his lips distracted me momentarily. Long enough that I didn't notice right off the way his iridescent golden eyes had trailed from my breasts to my Kate Spades, then back up to meet my eyes.

"Nice to meet you, Luciana Wagner. I'm Benjamin Snowden. You can call me Ben."

I smiled, transfixed by his killer grin and perfect white teeth. My mother would've loved his teeth.

Keeping my tone polite, I replied with, "You can call me Luci." But what I was thinking was, "You can call me anything you'd like, just as long as you call me."

Rein it in, Luci.

"And these are my partners," Ben noted, turning toward the others but not releasing my hand. He pointed to the blond. "Justin Parker." His hand swiveled over to the twins. "Landon and Langston Moore."

"Very nice to meet you all." With a smile on my face, I reached out and shook each man's hand once Ben released me. I kept my grip firm but feminine. I didn't want them to think I was trying to overpower them or anything.

That, of course, got me to thinking about being overpowered by them. Don't ask me why.

And suddenly, the room had heated about fifteen degrees.

Should've nixed the blazer.

Two

"IF YOU WOULD FOLLOW US, we'll set you up in the conference room," Justin said, his voice deep but clear, with an authoritative ring to it. I didn't detect an accent of any kind.

I met his smoldering blue eyes and nodded.

Turned out, I only ended up following Justin while the other three pulled up the rear. They resumed their conversation from the elevator, which, from what I could tell, was a rundown of their meetings for the day. I briefly wondered whose calendar the interview was on.

Justin stopped at a tall glass door, inserted a key to unlock it, then pushed it open. He allowed me to precede him, so I stepped into the room.

I was right about the windows. They ran the length of the room—floor to ceiling—and didn't have blinds to obstruct the view. The *awesome* view, I might add. The conference table that sat in the center and filled about three quarters of the space looked to hold roughly fifty people on a good day. I'd never seen anything like it. It was very modern with an opaque-glass top that appeared to be several inches thick. The chairs were black leather, all executive style. I had to wonder how many clients they had in there at a time. That seemed like a lot to me.

"A few times a year, we fly all of our managers in for meetings," Justin informed me, apparently reading my mind.

A lot of employees, then. I nodded and tucked that information away for later use.

Landon—I could tell the difference because he was wearing glasses and his twin was not—pulled out a chair and I mumbled my thanks as I slipped into it, careful to keep my skirt from riding up too far. As it was, I was baring quite a bit of thigh and the last thing I wanted was for them to think that I'd done it on purpose.

"Can we get you anything? Coffee? Tea? Water?" Langston offered. Now, he *did* have an accent, a sexy twang that hinted at his down-home roots. It wasn't local, I knew that much.

"I'm good, thank you." I felt as though I should've been offering them something, but I refrained. I would save that for my first day on the job. And no, I wasn't talking about offering up my body. Although…

"Would you mind giving us a few minutes?" Justin requested.

"No, not at all." I kept my tone sweet, meeting each of their eyes in turn.

I watched as all four men then walked out of the room.

"D-*ay*-um, Kristen. Where have you been hiding these guys?" I whispered to myself, then quickly jerked my gaze up to the corners of the room.

I was wondering if they had surveillance cameras. *And yep, lookie there.* They did. Several, in fact. Which meant I should probably stop ogling and undoubtedly stop muttering to myself.

Keeping my back straight and my hands tucked into my lap, I continued my perusal of the room. Aside from the ginormous table, there were three couches in this room also. These were black leather with neatly squared cushions, set in the same U formation as those in the lobby. Rather than facing a desk, though, they were positioned in front of a projection screen on the wall. Seemed like a good place to go through presentations to me.

Unlike the lobby, where the tiled floors were a dark gray rectangle in an offset pattern, the floors in here were big, oversized squares, neatly aligned and gleaming white.

Black, white, and chrome seemed to be the theme in this room.

It seemed a little sterile to me. On the other hand, it was professional. If it were mine, I would've decorated it with a few bright-colored floral decorations. Something to draw the eye and give a little life to the place.

Several minutes passed and I fought the urge to fidget, hyperaware of the cameras. I wanted to make a good impression, not look like I was ready to bolt at a moment's notice.

When the door opened again, Ben was the one who stepped inside. His smile was still firmly on his face, and I was still transfixed by it. He carried himself like a man who was comfortable in his own skin. The smile came across as warm and friendly, which instantly put me at ease.

"Are you sure I can't get you anything?" His voice was deep and it suited him nicely. No accent either.

Unless you're on the menu, then no.

"I'm sure. But thank you." I effectively ignored my inner hussy.

His charcoal suit highlighted his dark skin and looked spectacular on him. I could only imagine how nice his butt looked in those slacks without the jacket. Not that I was looking.

Fine, I *had* looked, but my attempt hadn't been successful.

He nodded, then took the seat directly across from me and placed a manila folder on the table.

Crap.

I didn't bring an extra copy of my resume. I knew I had forgotten something that morning.

Ben opened the folder and relief hit me like a tsunami. The first sheet was a copy of my resume. I was happy to see it for two reasons. One, it proved they were expecting me. And two, I forgot the extra one.

"Why don't you start by telling me a little about yourself, Luci."

Smoothing my hands over my skirt, I forced myself to maintain eye contact while making a concerted effort not to look constipated. Although I should've been a pro at these things by now, interviews weren't my forte. I got nervous, I sweated in places I shouldn't sweat, and I had a hard time speaking. Put me in front of a super-hot guy and it got doubly worse.

"As you can see by my resume, I have a significant amount of reception experience," I said, keeping my voice even, cheerful.

Ben's smile widened. "How about a little about you first. I'm more than aware of your work experience."

"Oh." That took me somewhat by surprise. "Like what? I mean, what would you like to know?"

"What are your hobbies? Where did you grow up? Those types of things."

Although his voice sounded professional, there was something in his eyes that said he would prefer to know my bra size. Then again, I could've been imagining that because I wanted to show him my bra so he could find the size himself.

Wait.

No I didn't.

I was no hussy.

Not like you could put a handsome man in a suit in front of me and my hormones took the reins.

Okay, they did.

That probably had a lot to do with the fact that I was single and the only orgasms I'd had in the past, oh, I don't know, two years had been from my trusty vibrator. Well, to be honest, it had been *two* vibrators. I wore the first one out completely. I had always had a powerful sex drive, but I was quite adept at sating my own urges. Porn and my vibrator were my two best friends, I wasn't ashamed to admit it.

Shit.

I was mentally off topic and now Ben was staring at me, his honey-gold eyes reflecting what I could only assume was amusement. If he knew what was going on in my head, I'm not sure he'd be smiling.

I took a deep breath, let it out.

What were my hobbies? Probably shouldn't tell him about porn and my vibrator.

So, that meant I had to go with the growing up part.

"I grew up not far from here," I told him. "My mother's a dentist, my stepfather's a firefighter—he adopted me when I was six—my real father died when I was three and I don't really remember him. I have no siblings, and they wouldn't let me have a pet growing up, but now I live in an apartment, still don't have a pet because I don't have time for one, but that was up until three weeks ago, anyway." Yes, I was a rambling mess. "Technically, right now I have plenty of time since I don't have a job, but that's not to say I don't want one, because I definitely do—a job, not a pet—and as you can see, I've got a ton of reception experience."

This time Ben laughed, a dark, rich sound that dripped with sexiness and made me grateful I'd worn panties.

I replayed what I'd just said in my head and realized I sounded like a total moron.

Great.

Ben leaned forward, closed the folder, then got to his feet.

Shit.

Did I seriously just blow the entire interview with one ridiculously long run-on sentence? Well, *two* ridiculously long run-on sentences, to be fair. I had taken a breath in there somewhere. I think.

"Is the interview over?" I asked when he stepped away from the chair.

"Certainly not." His face was expressionless, his eyes assessing me again. "I'm going to have Mr. Parker come in. Then Langston and Landon. After they've all asked you a few questions, we'll convene and let you know."

"Oh." Okay then. I briefly wondered why he referred to one of his colleagues as mister but referred to the other two by their first names.

"It's been a pleasure to meet you, Luci."

"Thank you." When he shook my hand, this time I was reluctant to let go, but I forced my fingers to release his as he once again smiled down on me.

My brain suddenly conjured up an image of me on my knees and...

Oh.

My.

God.

I'd completely lost my mind.

•

By the time Mr. Parker—Justin—strolled into the conference room, I had managed to battle back the blush that heated my face when Ben was on his way out. I knew this because I had glanced at myself in the reflection of the table and it appeared I was as pale as I had been when I walked in the office.

Not that that would be the case once Mr. Parker began talking, but at least I got a clean slate to start from.

He didn't remain standing for long, so I only had a few seconds to take in the dark blue suit that emphasized his navy-blue eyes. He was taller and broader in the chest than Ben was, narrower in the hips as well, but I couldn't confirm on the butt because he, too, was wearing a jacket.

"I see you've held a multitude of jobs over the years."

"That's true," I agreed.

"Was there one that held your interest more than the others?"

I thought about that for a moment, then shook my head. "No, Mr. Parker, not that I can recall."

"Please, call me Justin."

Okay then.

"So, Luci, tell me a little about your experience at"—he opened the folder and skimmed the extensive list of companies I'd worked for—"um...Super Cuts?"

I smiled because this was the easy part. "I worked there for about three months as a receptionist back when I was just out of college. I answered phones and scheduled appointments. Sometimes they had me sweep the floor if I had nothing else to do."

Did I say *easy*?

I really meant lame because now that I heard myself, I was no longer wondering why no one was hiring me. Any idiot could work as a receptionist at Super Cuts if they were solely responsible for answering the phone and sweeping the floor. Sheesh.

Yes, Justin. I'm an idiot. But I take orders well.

I forced my mind not to wander because I felt Justin's eyes on me and I didn't want to imagine him ordering me to go to my knees.

Fuck.

I was completely out of control.

Someone shoot me now.

Before I could think of anything else to add, Justin leaned forward, closed the folder, then got to his feet.

Son of a bitch.

I was on a roll this morning.

Although Ben had assured me I would be meeting with all four of them, I wasn't sure that was the case any longer. After all, I *had* heard myself. I made eye contact with the handsome Justin and asked, "Is the interview over?"

"Not yet, no. I'm going to send Landon and Langston in. Once they've run through their questions, we'll meet and then let you know."

Okay, good. So that was still the plan. I felt a little better. Granted, this interview was a bit strange what with the lack of questions or details, but I figured I couldn't complain. They hadn't booted me out yet.

"Thank you for meeting with me." I shook his hand when he offered.

"My pleasure." He pivoted, then slipped out of the room.

"Okay, Luci. Time to make like Stella and get your groove on." I was no longer worried about the cameras overhearing me talking to myself. Wasn't like I could look more like an idiot than I already had.

I glanced over at the counter, noticing the bottles of water. Glass bottles. Fancy ones. The kind no one really drank, but they set out so they looked like they had class and money.

Not that I was doubting that these guys had either, but...

The door opened and I turned to see Landon and Langston coming in. Their suits were a conservative black, shirts a crisp white. Landon's tie was a deep burgundy while Langston's was a shimmering royal blue. They looked nice, professional. Sexy.

Langston grabbed one of the glass bottles of water and unscrewed the top before taking a sip, disproving my theory that they were only for show.

Landon sat down in the chair across from me and Langston perched his hip on the cabinet behind him. Both men seemed to be observing me intensely. I fought the urge to squirm under the scrutiny of their gazes. It wasn't easy, especially when my eyes met Langston's. There was something about that man, something that made me think of smoking-hot sex.

Finally, Landon spoke. "What makes you think you're qualified for this position?"

He had the type of deep, raspy voice that single women wanted to hear whispering in their ear moments before they were rocketed into the ether riding the waves of an intense orgasm.

Yep. Flip me over. I'm done.

Landon's dark eyebrow lifted and I realized he was waiting for me to speak.

"Well…" I smiled, then my mouth ran away from me when I blurted, "I'm not sure how to answer that since I haven't the faintest clue what the requirements are."

"If you don't know the requirements, why'd you apply for the job?" His voice rang with amusement. And sex. Mostly sex.

Damn it.

That wasn't him, that was me.

I didn't want to tell them that I applied because my friend told me I should. That didn't seem very responsible. It wasn't like I was expecting to get it simply because I knew Kristen either. Sure, we'd become good friends over the past two years, but I certainly wasn't trying to ride her coattails. Then again, I wasn't above latching on and taking a short ride if it meant steady employment. Hell, the idea of having to live with my parents was enough to have my desperation ratcheting up a notch or twenty.

I kept the smile on my face. "Because I'm quite aware of the reputation of this company and I felt I would be a good fit here. I'm a hard worker, speak well with clients, and I'm looking for something to broaden my horizons."

"Very nice answer," Landon stated at the same time Langston muttered, "Good girl," from his spot near the wall, his hazel eyes pinned on me.

There was something about the way he said that. Something that made me want to continue to have him praising me in the future. Like I said, I was losing my mind. But hey, I'd already dug a deep enough hole to hide in; what was the point in trying to climb out now?

Unlike Ben and Justin, Landon didn't open the folder.

"Tell me how you know Kristen Morrow."

Okay, so they evidently knew how I'd heard about the job, and I had to assume that they knew her as well since they were the only ones who'd asked about her. "She's a friend of mine," I admitted. "We met at yoga class a couple of years ago. We hang out from time to time."

My answer seemed to placate them.

"I noticed you have a degree in accounting." Landon's eyes scanned my face as he spoke.

"That's true, I do."

I'd been told to never provide additional information that they didn't require because it overshadowed the interview and if they weren't in need of an accountant, what did it matter anyway?

"Are you interested in the secretary position, Luci?" Langston asked.

"Yes, sir. I'm actually interested in *any* position."

Jeezus. Did I really just say that?

There was a flash of something in Langston's eyes that instantly had me crossing my legs a little tighter, a welcome ache taking up residence between my thighs. Well, it would've been a welcome ache if I weren't in a job interview. And if I had my trusty second vibrator handy.

"We work Monday through Friday," Landon told me. "You'd be required to be here from seven thirty to five thirty. An hour for lunch. We shut the office down at one on Fridays, but we do require one Saturday a month. My partners and I don't arrive until closer to eight. One or more of us is often traveling, so it would be critical that you be able to manage your time and your duties with little instruction from us."

I nodded. I could handle those hours and those requirements, despite the fact that I'd be getting up at the ass-crack of dawn every day.

"We each have extensive teams who work remotely. Rarely will you see anyone else in the office. However, we are a client-facing business, so the dress code is professional. What you're wearing is certainly appropriate."

"With one exception," Langston noted.

My gaze shot to his face as I waited for him to elaborate.

"Your skirts should be no shorter than the tips of your fingers when your arms are hanging at your sides. Anything shorter would be considered indecent and grounds for...discipline."

I had no idea why the word discipline coming from that delectable mouth sounded so naughty, but it did.

"Yes, sir. Fingertip length."

"Otherwise, your attire is appropriate," he concluded.

Still, that meant I would have to go shopping because this was the extent of my professional wardrobe. I hadn't been required to dress up at Super Cuts or Home Depot or Target. When I'd done a brief stint as a receptionist at my mother's dental office, she insisted I wear scrubs. Those few weeks I had tried my hand at waitressing a couple of years back, Hooters had supplied the uniform.

But I had this. Fashion was totally my thing.

"Are you available to start immediately?" Landon inquired, once again taking control of the interview.

"Yes, sir. I am."

His response was a gravelly grunt that sounded like approval.

Now that I was used to it, I didn't panic when Landon got to his feet, this time grabbing the folder.

"If you'll excuse us for a few minutes, I'd like to discuss with my partners."

"Sure you don't want some water?" Langston offered.

"I'm sure." It was a lie. My mouth was parched, but I was too nervous to drink anything.

"We'll be back in a minute," Landon noted, then disappeared into the hallway, his twin following him.

I kept my eyes on them, which was the only reason I saw Langston wink at me.

That or he had something in his eye.

When the door closed, I stared at it for a minute, replaying that scene over in my head.

Yep. Definitely a wink.

It got warm again.

I'm too young for hot flashes, right?

I tried to relax, but it was nearly impossible.

Waiting was the worst part. Although, I realized, most of the interviews I'd been on had ended with a follow-up call to let me know I wasn't selected for the position, so there hadn't been a lot of waiting. From what I could tell, they were planning to give me the news before I left the building.

So, was that a good thing? Or bad? Face-to-face rejection seemed like it would be significantly more uncomfortable than over the phone.

I didn't have time to think about that before all four men stepped back into the conference room. They were intimidating on their own. Together they were a force to be reckoned with. And it was hard not to stare.

Ben moved over to me first and I jerked my gaze to his face.

"Luci, we'd like to offer you the job if you're interested. Here's the information on the position," he said, handing me a small sheet of paper, which listed out the salary information. "It also comes with full benefits, vacation, et cetera."

I nodded, smiling as I looked back up at him. "Yes, sir. I'm definitely interested."

"Good." He clasped my hand and helped me to my feet. "We'd like for you to start immediately. Will tomorrow morning work for you?"

"Absolutely."

"We'll expect you here at seven thirty."

I nodded again.

The next thing I knew, the four men were leading me back toward the elevator.

It wasn't until I was on my way down to the first floor that I realized I never did find out what the requirements were.

Three

BOSS MEETING

LANGSTON

"OKAY, NOW THAT WE'VE OFFICIALLY hired her, tell me your thoughts," Justin prompted when we sat down in the conference room not two minutes after the elevator doors closed behind Luci.

Truthfully, I would've preferred to get coffee before we had this discussion.

"Before we get to that," Landon interrupted, "where's Jordan?"

"He had an appointment this morning," Ben confirmed. "Didn't say where, but I also didn't ask. Said he'd be in around eleven."

Landon frowned. "Didn't look great that we had no one in the office when she arrived."

It was obvious my twin wasn't impressed by the way we'd greeted our new employee, and I could understand his point. Good thing she'd decided to accept the job. Landon might've been the most laid-back of the four of us—well, except maybe Ben—but he was a stickler for etiquette. And he was right, we had failed in that regard.

Again, coffee would've been good right about now.

Justin nodded. "I agree. However, it's not like we had anyone to fill in for him."

Okay, so Justin had a good point, too. Sort of.

"And what? We're too good to come in early or answer the phones?" Landon huffed. "I woulda volunteered if I'd known."

Yeah. Not me. I didn't have the patience to man the front desk. Nor the desire.

We'd been down a secretary for the past week and a half. Getting someone in wasn't as easy as it looked. For one, we were looking for someone specific, someone who could manage the office, maintain a certain amount of decorum, not provide a lot of drama, and be open to future possibilities. Not to mention, get along with our remote employees and give our CPA guidance as needed.

To be fair, we had interviewed both men and women, although we weren't looking to hire a man. Not for this position anyway.

Needless to say, it had been hit or miss thus far and every time we seemed to find someone we all four agreed on, she was out the door within a couple of weeks tops. Apparently, we were rather intimidating, or so I'd heard.

But enough was enough. I was tired of talking about the empty office or who was willing to do what. So I decided to push things along since coffee was my first order of business.

"She came with a great recommendation from Kristen," I told them, leaning back in my chair and regarding my partners. It was far too early to be having this conversation—or any, for that matter—but even I couldn't think of a better time. The girl would be starting in the morning and it was pertinent that we were on the same page when it came to what she'd be doing.

"I'll admit," Landon began, "she didn't look at all like what I expected her to."

Unlike my brother, I hadn't had any expectations. Five feet two inches with light blue eyes, long, dark hair with a massive amount of highlights, and a heart-shaped ass were all good as far as I was concerned.

"Good or bad?" Justin's eyes held the question his lips spoke.

We all turned to Landon. "For one, she's younger than I thought she'd be."

Justin peered down at the notebook in his hand. "Her application says she's twenty-four."

I frowned. "I thought we weren't allowed to ask questions like that."

"It asks for date of birth." Justin's tone was defensive.

"She certainly caught my attention." We all knew what Ben was referring to.

Although we ran a respectable, multimillion-dollar business, there was no denying that we had a few idiosyncrasies. For example, we lived and breathed Dominance and submission. It wasn't merely a fetish, D/s was a lifestyle choice for each of us.

On top of that, we were all looking to find a woman we could...share. Perhaps it wasn't politically correct according to a lot of people, but it was what it was. I certainly wasn't about to apologize for it and I doubted my partners would either. And considering we spent the majority of our time in the office, we were looking for someone we could interact with in that particular setting. On more than a business level.

Not that we were solely willing to hire based on that. We had several positions we could fill and should the right person stumble upon us, we weren't opposed to finding them a spot.

"According to Kristen," Landon said, "she's a natural submissive."

"I got that just by talking to her," Ben noted.

Hell, I got it just by *looking* at her.

"Me, too," Justin confirmed. "How long has Kristen known her?"

"A couple of years," Landon supplied.

"Are they close?" Ben asked.

I sighed heavily. "I'm sorry, but we didn't interrogate Kristen about her friend. She mentioned that she knew someone who was right up our alley and she just so happened to be single *and* looking for a job. It seemed appropriate to have her nudge the girl in our direction."

Justin glanced between the three of us. "As with the others, we're going to have to give it some time, get to know her a little. Feel her out before we take the next steps."

"First and foremost," I said, drawing all eyes to me, "she has to be able to handle the responsibilities. Unlike the last woman you hired"—I glared over at Justin—"who didn't know how to properly answer a telephone."

"Or the one before that," Landon added, "who didn't know what email was."

"Regardless of our intentions," I continued, "we need someone who's competent in the office. I'm not willing to take anything less."

Justin rolled his eyes. "Point taken."

"Did anyone bother to ask her why she left her previous jobs?" Ben questioned. "Because she has an extensive list."

That she did.

I looked at each man in turn. No one said anything. Appeared as though we'd all been too tongue-tied to really find out the pertinent information. Not that anyone could blame us. Personally, I'd been quite taken by the girl. She was probably the most stunning woman I'd laid eyes on in a really long time. And yes, she had a sweet innocence about her that I'd instantly homed in on. I'd known as soon as I saw her that she would fit in here perfectly.

"Well, I found it interesting that she didn't ask about the job requirements," Landon said, smirking.

Ben grinned. "No, she definitely did not."

I cleared my throat and moved to get to my feet. "Well, I say we give her a month, see how she does. We'll reconvene after she's been here for a week to discuss where we're at. Unless something comes up that needs to be discussed before then."

Justin stood. "I'm good with that."

Ben and Landon both agreed.

Finally, we were going to get down to real business.

Coffee.

I needed caffeine before I dealt with anything else today.

Unfortunately, since we still lacked a secretary, I would have to make it myself.

About Nicole Edwards

New York Times and *USA Today* bestselling author Nicole Edwards lives in Austin, Texas with her husband, their three kids, and four rambunctious dogs. When she's not writing about sexy alpha males, Nicole can often be found with her Kindle in hand or making an attempt to keep the dogs happy. You can find her hanging out on Facebook and interacting with her readers - even when she's supposed to be writing.

Nicole also writes contemporary/new adult romance as Timberlyn Scott.

Website
www.NicoleEdwardsAuthor.com

Facebook
www.facebook.com/Author.Nicole.Edwards

Twitter
@NicoleEAuthor

By Nicole Edwards

The Alluring Indulgence Series
Kaleb
Zane
Travis
Holidays with the Walker Brothers
Ethan
Braydon
Sawyer
Brendon

The Austin Arrows Series
The SEASON: Rush
The SEASON: Kaufman

The Bad Boys of Sports Series
Bad Reputation
Bad Business

The Caine Cousins Series
Hard to Hold
Hard to Handle

The Club Destiny Series
Conviction
Temptation
Addicted
Seduction
Infatuation
Captivated
Devotion
Perception
Entrusted
Adored
Distraction

The Coyote Ridge Series
Curtis
Jared

The Dead Heat Ranch Series
Boots Optional
Betting on Grace
Overnight Love

The Devil's Bend Series
Chasing Dreams
Vanishing Dreams

The Devil's Playground Series
Without Regret
Without Restraint

The Office Intrigue Duet
Office Intrigue
Intrigued Out of the Office
Their Rebellious Submissive

The Pier 70 Series
Reckless
Fearless
Speechless
Harmless

The Sniper 1 Security Series
Wait for Morning
Never Say Never

The Southern Boy Mafia Series
Beautifully Brutal
Beautifully Loyal

Standalone Novels
A Million Tiny Pieces
Inked on Paper

Writing as Timberlyn Scott
Unhinged
Unraveling
Chaos

Naughty Holiday Editions
2015
2016

Made in the USA
Monee, IL
16 April 2020